Love Dies In The End
Eliza Arabi

Dedications:

To my mom, who's been my rock, my backbone, my biggest fan, and the woman I would set the world on fire for.

To Reem, my partner in crime, therapist, and the one who gets all my weird, existential rants while somehow making sense of them. You make life feel like a chaotic, beautiful mess, and I wouldn't want it any other way.

To A, the MVP of this book. You're the one who stayed up way too late downloading 10,000 apps for the perfect edits and kept me from tossing my laptop out the window. You've been the unsung hero of every design, location idea, and transition. You listened to me drone on and on about chapters, and somehow, you still didn't run for the hills. You're the real one.

To Soukaina, my boss, who somehow managed to be a ray of sunshine in the middle of the storm. You're the kind of person who makes it feel like I could handle anything, even when I'm questioning my life choices. Thank you for being the safe space I didn't know I needed.

To Priscillah and Ayah, the dynamic duo who kept me sane in the middle of the madness. You two are the best kind of chaos—sipping matcha, spilling tea, and making sure I never forget that life is too short to take it seriously. You'll forever be my therapy in human form.

To my artistic friend Hind, whose creativity and strength amidst the daily battles have shown to be admirable.

Lastly, to my dad, who I lost before I could become so much more than the chaos he knew....I miss you every day and I wish you had been here to see how much love I am surrounded by.

Without you all, this book wouldn't have been more than a wild idea in my head. You kept me going when it felt impossible, and for that, I'll never be able to thank you enough.

"The villain's lip curled, a sneer twisting their features.

'Choose your last words. Make them count.'

A tremor shook the hero, but their gaze remained unwavering.

'I loved you,' they breathed, a fragile defiance.

A flicker of something like pain crossed the villain's eyes.

'And I loved you...,' they hissed, the words raw and broken.

'But here, on this blood-soaked field, love is a death sentence.'

The villain's hand tightened on the trigger, knuckles bone-white.

A single, sharp crack ripped through the air.

The hero fell, and with them, the last vestige of the villain's shattered humanity.

The echo of the gunshot was a funeral dirge for a heart they had just destroyed."

Chapter 1:

Silver, Delicate, and Tarnished

Fog clung to the alleyway, as if it had rooted itself into the cracked pavement and filth-streaked brick walls, refusing to be moved. It drifted in a slow, serpent like pattern, swallowing the neon signage until only faint, ghostly halos remained—hovering above like disinterested witnesses to something irreversible. Yellow crime-scene tape fluttered ineffectually in the wind, a fragile border drawn too late, trying to contain a moment that had already etched itself into permanence. Camera flashes broke through the gloom in sharp bursts, lighting up fragments of the scene. Rusted dumpsters stood like forgotten sentinels, oil-slick patches gleamed on the pavement, and the unmistakable outline of a body rested beneath a white sheet.

The air reeked of bleach and blood, the metallic tang of iron mingling with the sharp sting of chemicals. The smell crept into your lungs, settled deep in your throat, and refused to release its grip even long after you had left. It clung not just to your clothes, but to your very memory.

Love stood just beyond the police line, breath caught somewhere high in her chest, where it couldn't seem to move past her collarbones. Her heart pounded with such force she could hear it reverberate in her ears, a deep, hollow thud that drowned out the rising voices of first responders, the distant wail of sirens, and the slow grind of stretcher wheels over gravel. Then the wind lifted the edge of the sheet—only for a moment, but long enough.

The overhead light revealed a pale, small, and slack wrist, the skin translucent in its halogen wash. Love knew that wrist. She could trace its freckled curve from memory. A responder lunged to cover it again, but the damage was done. Her eyes had already found the bracelet—silver, delicate, slightly tarnished. Three charms: a chipped music note, a lopsided heart, and a tiny book with the spine rubbed smooth from years of wear. Childhood relics from a summer spent making promises with glitter glue and giggles, vowing never to take them off—not for swimming, not for sleepovers, not even for school picture day.

Now, the bracelet clung to a corpse, and the promise meant nothing.

She moved before she realized it, boots crunching across glass, shoving past officers who called her name with rising urgency. Someone grabbed her arm, but she twisted away.

"Ophelia!" Her voice cracked open the night like lightning striking dry wood.

Red curls spilled from beneath the sheet.

Her knees gave out. Her world tilted sideways, and her scream collapsed into silence.

Everything went dark.

&a &a &a &a &a &a &a

When she woke, she was gasping, drenched in sweat, tangled in sheets that had coiled around her legs like vines. The room held too much light. Sunlight cut across the walls in aggressive slashes, slicing the shadows like interrogation lamps. A lavender candle burned low on her nightstand, its scent heavy and sweet, cloying in a way that made her stomach turn.

Downstairs, voices collided like storm fronts.

"She wouldn't have hidden it if she trusted you."

"And you think she told you everything?"

Her parents. Again. Still trying to dress their grief in accusation, their anger clinging to every word like static. Still too proud to bleed openly. Still too scared to sit still with their sorrow.

Love pulled on a lilac sweater, oversized and soft at the edges from too many wash cycles. Ophelia's favorite to tease her for. She didn't bother brushing her hair. Copper strands, tousled and uneven, fell around a face that looked more like a war monument than a girl—hollow-eyed, grieving, tired.

When she descended the stairs, the voices ceased instantly. Her mother stood by the counter, eyes red-rimmed and raw. Her father sat rigid at the kitchen table, staring at the far wall like it held a better version of the day.

"I'm leaving," Love said.

"Love—"

"Don't stop on my account." Her voice was flat, but the bitterness beneath it cracked. "And don't pretend like you both didn't help build the storm that killed her."

She didn't slam the door. She let it close gently, the silence behind it far louder than any bang could be.

Her car sat waiting in the driveway, a dust-coated matte black Corolla that had seen better decades. The engine still turned over with a low purr when she turned the key. Stickers lined the back window, their edges curled and faded from years of sunlight—souvenirs from road trips, inside jokes reduced now to static shapes and peeling glue. The glove-box wouldn't close properly. The passenger seat bore a small tear in the fabric that Ophelia had once tried to patch with embroidery thread that clashed entirely with the upholstery.

Love gripped the steering wheel but didn't move. The car idled, air vents hissing with old breath.

The passenger seat was empty.

But not really.

Ophelia lived there, now. Not in body, but in shadow. In echo. Head tucked into the hoodie, feet propped up on the dash, curls a mess of red knots, a straw from some forgotten smoothie still between her teeth. Love could almost hear her again.

"Why do you always play sad girl music?"

"It's thematic," Love would say, smiling sideways.

Ophelia would roll her eyes, call her insufferable, then change the song to something equally tragic.

They used to drive for hours, windows cracked to let the cold in, narrating the lives of strangers in other cars, and laughing about things that didn't matter. They talked about love like it was a foreign country.

Now, the seat was empty. Somehow, the absence was heavier than her presence ever was.

Love touched the cupholder. It was cold. Of course it was.

She put the car in gear and drove.

✧ ✧ ✧ ✧

Campus looked unchanged. Snow still lined the sidewalks in dirty, uneven patches. Students passed in clumps, laughing, shouting, living like the world hadn't caved in. No one looked at her long enough to register her grief. That part almost hurt more.

The library was safer. Its corners were hushed. The farthest table in the back still remembered the weight of her elbows. She opened her laptop and stared at the blinking cursor like it owed her something. A sticky note clung to the edge of the screen, its ink faded from sun and touch:

"The greatest loss isn't death. It's what dies inside us while we're still alive."

Her pen hovered. But the words stayed trapped behind her teeth.

Then her phone buzzed.

Layla.

"Party tonight. You're coming. I already picked your outfit."

"I don't—"

"Don't think. Just go. You'll stand in the corner looking like some tragic masterpiece. People will stare. They'll whisper. You'll hate every second. But it'll still beat staying home."

The line cut off before she could answer.

The night swallowed the sky. No stars, just clouds stretched taut and halogen lamps casting dull pools of orange onto the pavement. At the end of the block, the house pulsed with bass, a living thing. Windows glowed like stained glass in a church of the godless. Laughter spilled onto the street—shrill, fractured, careless. The kind that made you feel more alone when you heard it.

Love stood across the street, breath fogging in front of her, hands tucked into the deep pockets of her coat. The world was still spinning. Still unaware that her sister was gone. Still indifferent.

She loathed parties. The noise, chaos, and superficial connections were unbearable, but the silence tonight was far more disturbing. Recently, the silence had become a slow, painful demise.

So she crossed the street.

Not because she wanted to.....

It's because she couldn't go back home. Not yet. Not to the place where grief sat like an unwanted guest at every table, in every corner. And not to the silence that knew her name too well.

Chapter 2:

I *Walk Into Fires*

Love sat on the cold stone bench just outside the house, her arms wrapped tightly around herself while the wind tugged at the hem of her dress like a restless ghost. The night wasn't just cold — it was biting. It gnawed at her skin in little, invisible teeth, the kind that didn't leave marks but hollowed you out slowly. Through the windows, flashes of light revealed people laughing and swaying, their silhouettes melting together in bursts of motion. Inside, the world felt full — music and heat and lives being lived at full volume. Out here, there was only quiet. Stillness. Her.

She exhaled through her nose, breath curling in the air like a ghost trying to escape her lungs. It made everything feel unnecessarily cinematic.

"You're really doing this?" she mumbled under her breath, her voice low. "Brooding outside like some haunted Victorian extra?"

The corners of her mouth twitched at her own sarcasm, but it didn't quite reach her eyes. She stood before she could spiral further, brushing her hands down the fabric of her dress like that would iron out the ache in her chest. The gravel path crackled beneath her steps as she approached the door, each movement a quiet rebellion against the inertia that had been holding her still all week.

The bass grew louder as she neared the entrance, each vibration syncing with her heartbeat in a rhythm that felt more like a warning than a welcome. This wasn't her scene. Not tonight. Layla had insisted, coaxing her with half-laughed promises and glitter-lined eyes. A quiet part of her had allowed it. The part still clinging to the idea that noise could cure numbness.

She stepped closer, drawn to the chaos like a moth that didn't care if the flame burned. The silence she carried had grown heavy, settling behind her eyes, whispering in every pause between breaths. She needed to be swallowed by something louder than her own thoughts.

Inside, the music pulsed like a second heartbeat. People danced like they had never been hurt.

She envied them for a moment.

Then she walked in.

As she opened the door reluctantly, warmth spilled out and wrapped around her like a too-tight hug. Laughter and perfume clashed in the air, the kind of atmosphere that stuck to your skin and made your lungs work harder. The house was alive with bodies pressed too close, strangers orbiting each other in a haze of intoxication and glitter. Someone's hand brushed her back. Another offered her a drink she didn't want. She weaved through the crowd like a thread being pulled through cloth, ducking offers and side steps, until—

A hand found her elbow.

"Earth to Love." Layla's voice rang like a bell through the noise, clear and bright with mischief. She looked like a walking rebellion against minimalism — wild dark curls pulled back with rhinestone clips, combat boots paired with a sequined sweater dress, glitter dusting her collarbones like she'd wrestled a unicorn and won.

"You look like you've seen a ghost."

"Not a ghost," Love said, dryly. "Just the crushed remnants of my will to live."

Layla snorted, the sound unapologetic. "And here I was, hoping you'd be the "fun" kind of sad tonight."

Love took one look at her friend's eyeliner — uneven wings, unapologetically bold — and almost laughed. Leave it to Layla to look like a glitter-soaked prophet at the end of the world.

"Sorry. Existential dread doesn't dance."

Layla ignored that, looping their arms together like she could physically steer her into a better mood. "Too bad. Ophelia would've dragged your sad ass into the middle of the room by now and made you do the worm."

Love gave a faint smile. "She also thought glitter body lotion was subtle."

"God, I miss her," Layla whispered, the weight of it slipping into the space between them.

"Me too," Love replied, and this time the silence they stood in wasn't cold. It was reverent. Grief, after all, was the only thing louder than music.

Something shifted. A flicker at the edge of her senses. Love's spine prickled with the distinct sensation of being watched, as if someone's gaze had brushed her skin like a fingertip. She turned slowly, eyes scanning the crowd until they landed on him.

She noticed him near the far wall, a figure set slightly apart from the pulse of the crowd, his posture calm but alert—as though he wasn't ignoring the chaos, just entirely unaffected by it.

He didn't sway to the beat, and didn't pretend to enjoy the noise. He stood with the quiet confidence of someone who didn't need to prove he belonged, like he was watching a storm he'd already outlived.

There was no tension in his stance, only a stillness that drew attention without asking for it. His gaze cut through the room with an unsettling kind of focus—not loud or lingering, but direct enough to make her pulse hitch. It wasn't the kind of look you stumble into. It was deliberate. Chosen.

When their eyes met, it felt less like being seen and more like being recognized—like he already knew what she looked like when she cried, when she lied, when she stopped pretending to be fine.

"Layla," she said under her breath, not breaking the gaze. "Who's that?"

Layla followed her line of sight and grinned. "Him? No idea. Showed up twenty minutes ago, like he owned the place. Gave off big Bond villain energy."

"Yeah," Love murmured. "I see it."

Before Layla could launch into another theory, Love was already moving. Her steps betrayed the hesitation she hadn't yet admitted, drawn forward by something magnetic and unspoken. Curiosity pulled at her ribs, and caution had long since excused itself from the evening.

When she reached him, he looked up. The smile that greeted her was measured and confident, unfolding with quiet precision. It didn't seek attention or approval. It simply existed—calm, unwavering, and sure of its place in the world. His eyes didn't just glance over her. They paused. They stayed. They read.

"You've been staring," he said, voice low and smooth, like velvet dipped in smoke. "Not that I blame you. It's a good view."

Love tilted her head, unimpressed. "You must get lonely being this obsessed with yourself."

"Only when I'm not being admired by beautiful women who glare like I've wronged them in a past life."

"I'm glaring because you're standing like someone's about to paint you."

He stepped closer, closing the space between them with deliberate ease. "Would you?"

"Only in red," she answered, "and only because I'd run out of black."

His laugh was soft, a quiet thing that curled at the edges. "Alexei."

"Love."

He raised an eyebrow. "Fitting."

"I'm not reading into it," he said, and something in his smile shifted. "But it suits you. Sharp around the edges. Soft in the middle."

Then, slower, his eyes scanning her with that unsettling calm.

"You're... compact chaos, aren't you?" His voice dropped just a notch. "Like if anyone makes the mistake of underestimating you, they'd find out the hard way."

His gaze lingered for just a beat — respectful, but unmistakably intrigued.

"Power in a small package. That's dangerous."

She gave a dramatic sigh. "Do you flirt like this with everyone, or am I just extra lucky?"

"I don't flirt," Alexei said, and something in his smile shifted. "I observe. I respond. And I ask the questions people usually run from."

"What kind of questions?"

"Like what makes a woman dress like she's untouchable and walk like she dares someone to prove otherwise?"

That stopped her cold.

For a second, the room dimmed. Or maybe it was just her pulse drowning out the noise. There was something unsettling about the way he looked at her, not as if he wanted to impress her, but as if he already knew the parts she tried to hide.

He held out his hand. No pressure. Just a quiet, steady offer.

She hesitated....but only for a moment.

Her fingers met his, and together, they slipped from the crowd. Through the kitchen, down a hallway that had none of the party's glow. The corridor was narrow and dim, lit only by the occasional flicker of string lights. He pushed open a door she hadn't noticed before and stepped aside to let her in first.

The room was small, almost bare. A bed, desk, and a single lamp casting gold across the floor. The night whispered in through the cracked window. It smelled like old pages and something faintly herbal.

Stillness settled over them.

"Last chance to leave," he murmured, voice softer now, closer to something honest.

"I don't leave," she said, quiet but steady. "I walk into fires."

He touched her hair gently, brushing it behind her ear like it was a ritual. "Then burn with me."

She did.

The kiss did not ask permission. It arrived like a storm breaking after too many days of silence, mouth on mouth like a question answered too late. There was no hesitation, no politeness in the way their hands moved, desperate and deliberate, fingers skimming over fabric that suddenly felt too heavy, too false. Buttons slipped open beneath trembling palms, and the distance between them unraveled—not neatly, but frantically, as if undone by gravity itself.

They didn't remove clothing. They stripped away the layers that had kept them contained. Her breath caught as his hand found the hollow of her back. His pulse surged when her lips grazed his neck. They devoured each other slowly, reverently, like hunger that had waited too long to speak its name.

It wasn't just need. It wasn't just grief. It was something stranger, deeper—born of shared shadows, sleepless nights, words unsaid, and the ache of being understood too late. Every touch asked a question. Every gasp was an answer. They moved together as if they had always been headed toward this moment, a single thread pulling tighter and tighter until neither of them could breathe without the other.

It was not perfect. It was not clean, but it was real. That, for both of them, was enough to make it holy.

◈ ◈ ◈ ◈

As the room fell into silence and their breathing evened out, Love traced slow shapes along his chest with the tip of her finger. He was warm, far too warm for someone who felt like a stranger. She wanted to ask him things she shouldn't. Wanted to know if he'd ever made anyone else feel like this — like gravity had shifted in his direction.

"Did you know Russian cats sometimes get jury duty?" he said suddenly, voice half-asleep.

Love blinked, surprised. "What?"

"True story. My cat once got summoned. He ignored it."

She laughed, letting it tumble from her like something trapped behind her ribs all night. "What's his name? Comrade?"

"Boris Mikhailovich. He takes no orders."

Love smiled. "Maybe I'll like him more than I like you."

"He's certainly fluffier."

He brushed a hand down her spine, slow and certain. Neither of them said anything more. And when she finally let her eyes close, it wasn't exhaustion that pulled her under. It was something gentler. Something that felt dangerously like trust.

◇ ❧ ◇ ❧ ◇

By morning, he was gone.

The sheets still held his warmth, but the man himself had evaporated — like mist, like a dream she wasn't sure she'd actually had. Love sat up slowly, the blanket slipping from her shoulders. The room looked unfamiliar in daylight, stripped of its shadows and mystery. Bare. Normal. Almost offensively ordinary.

She pressed her fingers to the spot beside her, half-expecting it to be cold, half-hoping it would be. If it was cold, maybe he'd never been there. Maybe it wouldn't matter so much that he was gone.

But it was warm.

Of course it was.

She swung her legs over the edge of the bed, every movement slow, as if rushing might shatter the fragile veil between night and morning, between feeling and forgetting. The surrounding silence wasn't peaceful. It rang in her ears like the moment after something breaks.

She wrapped the blanket around herself and wandered toward the window. The street below was empty — no signs of footsteps, no car door slamming in the distance, not even the trace of tire marks to chase. Just the soft gray light of a morning that didn't care how much had shifted in the dark.

Her eyes scanned the room once more, foolishly hopeful. Maybe he left a note. A number. A name that meant more than what he'd given her. Something real. Something solid.

Nothing.

Just the faint scent of his cologne lingering in the air, fading by the second.

She found her dress draped over the back of a chair — neat, intentional. Not tossed aside, not crumpled. Like someone had carefully returned it to her, like someone who didn't want to leave but had already decided he would.

Love closed her eyes.

This was the part she hated — the after. The unraveling. The questions that always come too late. Who was he, really? What had that night meant to him? And why did she feel as though a name she couldn't even spell had been carved into her chest?

She got dressed slowly, every movement careful, like she was getting ready to step back into a world that hadn't noticed her slipping out of it. And maybe it hadn't.

Her heels clicked faintly against the hardwood as she opened the door and stepped into the hallway. The sounds of the house had shifted. People were sleeping, or hungover, or quietly ghosting out of whatever version of themselves they'd worn last night.

She paused at the top of the stairs, one hand on the banister, her body still caught between questions and memory.

Then she heard it.

A laugh. Soft. Masculine. Familiar?

No, it couldn't be him. It was coming from downstairs, but it was too light. Too easy. Not the voice that had curled itself around her last night and dared her to burn.

She walked out without saying goodbye to anyone.

Outside, the cold slapped her skin, and this time she didn't shiver. She welcomed it. It reminded her that she was still here. That the night hadn't swallowed her whole. That maybe, just maybe, she still had choices left.

Just as she reached her car and slipped into the driver's seat, one thought kept replaying, looping quietly in the back of her mind like a haunting chorus:

He hadn't asked for her number.

He hadn't told her anything real.

Yet she felt like something had already begun...
something that wouldn't let her forget him.

✦ ❧ ✦ ❧ ❧ ✦ ❧ ❧ ✦ ❧ ❧ ✦ ❧ ❧

Chapter 3:

Immediate Exile

The clock above the library's main entrance was a massive, unblinking eye. Its hands crept forward with cruel indifference, each tick a quiet betrayal. Time wasn't healing anything. It was just dragging her further away from the last moment she remembered feeling whole.

Books sprawled across Love's desk like forgotten tombstones, their pages stained with highlighter and half-hearted notes. Shadows pooled in the gaps between their spines. The fluorescent lights above buzzed with that kind of exhaustion only libraries and hospitals could replicate — sterile and too bright, washing out color, warmth, and hope.

Midnight was still a few hours off, but her body had already surrendered. Her limbs ached with the heaviness of too many sleepless nights, and even breathing felt like it required negotiation. Every time she leaned closer to her notes, the words bled into each other, refusing to hold still. Her pen lay useless at her side. She hadn't written anything down in twenty minutes.

Layla, meanwhile, was a flurry of caffeine-fueled chaos. Her pen tore across the page with a vengeance, as if it had a score to settle. A faint smirk tugged at her mouth, suggesting she'd just thought of something funny only she would find amusing.

"You look like you're about to face plant into that textbook," she said, voice too loud for the quiet hum of the room.

Love didn't even lift her head. "Wouldn't be the worst thing to happen this week," she muttered. "At least it's soft."

Layla laughed, sharp and sudden. "You disappeared like a literal ghost at the party last weekend. What happened? And don't you dare hit me with the 'I was tired' excuse. I saw you. With him."

That got her attention. Love's gaze shifted from her textbook to Layla's raised eyebrows. She blinked once, then looked away. "It's... complicated."

"Complicated?" Layla leaned in like a journalist sniffing scandal. "Spill."

"I met someone," Love said, quieter now. The words felt fragile, like saying them out loud might ruin them. "We talked all night. It felt different. But then..."

She stopped. Pressed her fingers against her temple like she could press the memory back down where it belonged. "He was gone when I woke up. No note. No name. Just gone."

Layla's eyes widened. "He ghosted you after one night? Love, that's criminal. Jail. Immediate exile."

Love tried to smile, but it didn't stick. "It's fine. I'm fine."

"Babe." Layla reached over, her fingers grazing Love's arm. "You haven't been fine since Ophelia."

The name cracked something open.

Love didn't answer right away. She stared down at her notes, but the words had stopped meaning anything. She could feel the paper beneath her fingertips, but it might as well have been sand. Everything lately felt like it was slipping through her hands.

"She's still in every room," she whispered. "I keep thinking I'll hear her laugh around the corner. I keep having dreams where she's calling me and I can't move fast enough! And now this guy, this stranger, comes out of nowhere and it's like he sees every broken part of me. And I let him."

Layla didn't try to fix it. Instead, she just sat there with her silence steady. Her hand was still on Love's arm.

"You're allowed to let someone in," she said eventually. "Even if you're still hurting. You're human. You're not some machine that's supposed to power through loss and pretend to be fine just because other people are uncomfortable with grief."

Love closed her eyes. The lights above flickered again, casting the room in a split-second of shadow before buzzing back to life. Her chest felt tight, like something old and jagged had curled around her lungs and refused to let go.

"I need some air," she said abruptly, her voice thin.

Layla nodded, understanding immediately. "Want me to come?"

"No," Love said, already gathering her things. "I just... need to move."

The cold hit her like a slap the moment she stepped outside. Sharp wind cut across her cheeks, pulling tears to her eyes whether she wanted them or not. Her breath puffed out in uneven bursts, and her shoes clacked against the stone as she walked with no real direction. Just movement. Just the need to outrun whatever was clawing its way up her throat.

Campus looked different at night. Softer, quieter. The buildings looked like ancient sentinels, watching without judgment. Somewhere in the distance, a train wailed, long and mournful, slicing through the silence like it was delivering a message from somewhere far away.

She kept walking until the concrete turned to an uneven path and the noise of the streetlights gave way to crickets and wind. She didn't even remember choosing this direction. Her feet just carried her to the edge of campus, where a half-forgotten park still waited like a secret.

She found the bench beneath a crooked lamppost. The light above her flickered in intervals, casting weak halos on the sidewalk that didn't reach very far. She sat slowly, elbows on her knees, hands tangled in her hair. For a moment, she just breathed. In and out. In and out. Like it was the only thing anchoring her.

The silence refused to remain unbroken.

The memories always surfaced when she stopped moving. That night. The phone call. The moment the world tilted sideways and never set itself right again.

Her sister's name felt like grief and dust on her tongue. Ophelia. The police officers hadn't spoken it gently. They'd recited it as if reading from a script—detached, cold.

Your sister was found in an alley.

Found. As if she were a lost item, a misplaced object someone finally stumbled upon. Love had pictured the scene too many times. The wet pavement. The flashing lights. The way Ophelia's body must have looked, unnervingly still, unbearably wrong. She hated having to imagine it. She hated how easily she could.

Her stomach twisted.

She pulled her phone from her coat pocket. Her hand was shaking. She didn't even think about who to call. She just... needed someone who still tethered her to the world.

The screen lit up cold and blue. She scrolled. Found James.

When he answered, his voice was soft. Familiar. It caught her immediately, the way only someone who really knew you could. "Hey. What's going on?"

"I..." Her throat closed around the words for a second. "I need you. Can you come get me?"

No hesitation.

"Where are you?"

She looked around, her eyes scanning the shadowy shapes of trees and the worn path winding back toward the main road. "By the park. The one near the north edge of campus. You know the one with the sad little bench under the flickering street lamp?"

"I know it," he said. "I'll be there in fifteen."

She nodded, even though he couldn't see her. "Thanks."

When she hung up, she didn't move. She just sat there, listening to the hum of the streetlight and the quiet pulse of her own heart. It felt... real. Solid. Like something that still belonged to her.

Chapter 4:

M atching Crowns

James's car, a sleek black sedan that gave away nothing of the man behind the wheel, rolled to the curb like it had done it a hundred times before. The engine whispered low under the weight of the night, barely more than a breath. He stepped out without hesitation, every movement fluid and controlled. The air didn't dare push against him. His presence parted the cold like it recognized him.

Under the streetlights, his medium brown hair caught a faint shimmer, soft waves barely moving in the breeze. His skin looked pale beneath the November chill, and maybe it was the lighting, or maybe it was grief—either way, the color had drained from him in the way it does when life hits too hard and too fast.

His eyes, normally a calm and steady shade of green, carried a weight tonight. It wasn't fear or anger. It was a quiet concern that settles in your chest and refuses to leave.

He didn't call her name. He didn't ask where she'd been or why her coat hung around her like armor. He simply walked over to the park bench where she sat hunched under the flickering light and pulled her into his arms.

Love didn't resist. She didn't even think. She let herself collapse into the curve of him, into the familiarity that didn't demand anything. The wind tugged at her clothes and whipped her hair into a storm, but James held firm. One hand pressed against her back, his palm warm even through the layers, tracing slow, steady circles like he could rewrite the ache in her spine.

He didn't ask what was wrong.

He never had to.

"Come on," he whispered, his voice low and warm. "Let's get you home."

She nodded into his chest, not trusting her voice. The breath she took didn't ease the tightness, but it anchored her long enough to move.

The drive back to her house passed in a silence that didn't need to be filled. The heater hummed low; roads gilded beneath them in soft rhythm, and outside, Acadia Falls blurred into sleepy houses and leafless trees. Porch lights flickered past like ghosts. The sky above was a pale black, clouded and silent.

When they pulled into the driveway, neither of them moved right away. The porch light was off. The windows were dark, staring back at them like eyes that had seen too much and refused to blink.

James got out first and walked around to open her door. Love stepped out slowly, her legs stiff and her hands cold. Their shoes tapped against the steps, each sound a reminder of something shifting, something closing, and something about to unfold.

He opened the door for her, as if it wasn't just a gesture but a quiet assurance. As if he'd attuned himself to the cadence of her silence and knew exactly how to step into it.

The house swallowed them in stillness. There was no warmth, no glow, no soft music playing in the background. Just the weight of absence hanging heavy in every room.

Dahlia sat on the couch, her posture too straight to be comfortable. Her eyes were lined with exhaustion, but they softened the moment they landed on her daughter.

"Thank you for bringing her home," she said. Her voice was thin and cracked at the edges, like porcelain that had been glued back together too many times.

"Of course," James said, his voice steady and respectful. He nodded gently at her, not out of formality, but care.

Ashton stood from his chair with a kind of slow weariness that made Love's heart ache. His movements had grown heavier since the funeral. Like even standing upright demanded effort.

"I'll put on some tea," he offered quietly.

James gave a small smile. "That'd be great."

He moved into the kitchen without asking where anything was. He didn't need to. The cups were still in the second cabinet, just above the kettle. The tea bags were next to the sugar. He set the water to boil with practiced ease.

Everything about it was quiet. Routine. The kind of ritual you fall into when the world stops making sense and all you can do is go through the motions.

Love sat at the table, her arms resting on its surface, her eyes unfocused. The steam rose in slow curls once the water was poured. The mugs sat between them like offerings, something simple and warm to remind them they were still alive.

James made small talk, but it was gentle and brief. Just enough to keep the silence from closing in too tightly. He talked about the weather, a boring story from Channel 5, a headline about a new bookstore opening across town. None of it mattered, and that was the point.

He didn't try to pull her out of her grief.

He just sat with her in it.

Later, they moved into the living room. The coffee table was cluttered with open photo albums and half-folded tissue paper, like someone had been trying to find a memory and didn't know which one hurt least.

James picked up one of the albums. Its corners were worn, the cover slightly torn. He opened it gently, careful with each page until a photo stopped him.

Ophelia's last birthday. The kitchen behind her was decked out in pink and gold. Love stood beside her, cheeks flushed from laughing too hard. Her arms were wrapped around her sister, and their foreheads leaned together like they'd been carved from the same laugh.

"Remember this?" James asked, turning the page toward her.

Love leaned in. Her fingers hovered above the photo, brushing the edge but never quite touching it. "She always made a big deal about her birthday," she said, smiling faintly. "It was like a national holiday in her mind."

"She made us wear matching crowns."

"And sing the birthday song twice because the first one wasn't enthusiastic enough."

They turned the pages slowly, one after another. Time blurred between the photographs. Ophelia in the backyard blowing bubbles. In her cap and gown. At the beach, her sunburned nose and that ridiculous hat she refused to take off. Each image felt like a doorway to something they couldn't step back through, a memory too close, too raw.

James stayed patient. He didn't push. He never did. He had been there through every broken moment. When her world fell apart, he simply stayed. After the funeral, his uncle David Harrison arranged Love's internship at

Channel 5. James had asked him to. He thought it might help her find some solid ground, something to hold onto when everything else felt like quicksand.

For a while, it had.

Love's phone buzzed on the table. She glanced at it.

You okay? from Layla.

She typed back with thumbs that felt heavy:

With James. I'm fine. Thanks.

She turned the phone face down and looked at him.

"I can't move on," she said, barely more than a whisper. "Not until I know who did this to her."

James didn't flinch.

"I get it," he said softly. "But you can't let it eat everything else. You have to keep living, even while you're still looking."

She looked away. "Living," she repeated, as if the word didn't taste right in her mouth. "How do you live when the person who made life feel worth it is gone?"

"You fight," James said, without hesitation. "You fight by refusing to give whoever took her more than they already did. You fight for her memory, but you fight for yourself too."

She looked back at him then, really looked. His expression didn't carry pity. Just that quiet steadiness that had always grounded her. His hand slid across the table and found hers. He didn't squeeze. He just held it, warm and firm.

"You're not alone," he said. "You never were."

Love wanted to believe that. She almost did. But she was too tired to fight the doubt tonight. So she just nodded. It was enough for now. A quiet agreement with the universe to keep breathing.

James gave her hand a final squeeze and stood. He didn't grab his coat. Didn't say goodbye.

Instead, he walked into the kitchen and rinsed out their mugs, then flicked off the stove light. When he came back, he sat beside her on the couch and pulled the soft knit blanket from the armrest. Without a word, he draped it over her shoulders, then leaned back and stretched out, legs crossed, eyes distant.

Love curled up against the side of the couch, not quite touching him, but near enough to feel his presence. His breathing was steady, a quiet reassurance in a house that hadn't known peace in far too long.

They rested there, wrapped in a silence that carried no answers but eased the edges of the night. When sleep finally came, it didn't bring solutions, only a small measure of softness—enough to make tomorrow feel possible.

Chapter 5

Chasing Ghosts

The drive to the city archives felt less like a commute and more like a descent. With every mile, something in Love's chest pulled tighter, her nerves coiling in silence. The cracked leather of the steering wheel creaked under her grip, worn and brittle beneath her fingers. Outside, the November wind battered the windows in fitful bursts, cold and frantic, like it was trying to speak through the glass and couldn't form the words.

When she finally turned into the empty lot, the stillness settled around her like a second skin. The archives stood at the edge of the city like something left behind. Its structure was all hard lines and peeling paint, with windows that reflected nothing and a rusted sign that looked like it hadn't mattered in years. The building didn't welcome her. It waited. Silent. Braced.

Love lingered behind the wheel for a moment, staring at her hands. They looked pale in the dim light, stiff, unfamiliar. Like they belonged to someone else. Her breath fogged slightly in the air, and she let it hover there before reaching for the door handle and stepping into the cold.

Inside, the building smelled of old paper and time. The lighting buzzed overhead, humming in that sterile, tired way that made everything feel lonelier. Fluorescent light flattened every surface, casting strange shadows that clung to the floor like regrets. The air felt damp, not in the way of fresh rain but in the way of forgotten basements. Something about the scent made her stomach twist.

She knew where to go. She didn't wander. Her footsteps were soft and certain, the silence around her broken only by the faint hum of the vents.

She found the box quickly.

Ophelia Godfrey – Case Materials

Her sister's name, printed neatly in someone else's handwriting. She stared at it for a long moment. It didn't feel like reading. It felt like trespassing. The box was light in her hands, but its presence weighed more than it should have.

She opened it.

Inside, the past lay in disarray. Crime scene photos. Typed statements. Scanned police reports and autopsy notes. None of it was unfamiliar. She had seen it all before, in pieces. But reading it again wasn't about discovery. It was about penance. There was guilt sitting in her chest like a stone, and guilt doesn't loosen unless you revisit every last detail. Every failure. Every what-if.

She flipped through the contents slowly. Her hands trembled once, but she didn't stop. Something inside her was cold and quiet and determined.

And then, buried between pages of official phrasing and half-hearted observations, she saw it. One line. A note jotted in the corner of a witness account. Almost dismissive.

A dark sedan. High-end. No plates. Parked near the alley. Unfamiliar.

Her eyes locked on the words. She read them again. Then a third time. It wasn't a lead. Not really. It was a shadow. A whisper. But it was something. A thread so thin it felt like smoke, yet she folded the paper with care and slipped it into the inside pocket of her coat. It rested against her chest like a secret, small and sharp.

By the time she got home, the sky had deepened into a darker kind of blue. One that pulled at your thoughts. The kitchen lights were on. Warm and golden. Dahlia stood at the stove, wrapped in her favorite apron, the one with fraying ties and a faded floral pattern. Her back was turned. The scent of onions and cumin filled the room, rich and familiar.

"You went digging again," her mother said, not turning.

Love took off her coat and hung it near the door. "I just needed to check something."

Dahlia stirred whatever was in the pot. The motion was steady, precise. She turned her head just slightly, her expression unreadable. "And?"

"There was a car," Love said. "Parked near the alley that night. That's it."

Her mother didn't answer immediately. Her face remained calm, but her grip on the spoon tightened.

"You're chasing ghosts," she said, quietly.

"I'm chasing answers," Love murmured.

Ashton entered the room just then. His slippers shuffled softly across the tiles, and his robe was tied too tightly, as if holding himself together took effort. He looked at her gently, not with pity but with a kind of resignation.

"Answers or distractions?" he asked.

Love looked down at the floor. "Maybe both."

He didn't argue. He just nodded once and sank into his usual chair.

She didn't stay downstairs long. Her limbs were too heavy, and her mind too loud. She made her way up to her room and collapsed onto the bed, letting her body fall as if gravity had finally won. The mattress groaned under her, and the ceiling above stared back, blank and uncaring.

Her room had shrunk. That was the only way to explain it. The walls felt closer than they used to, like they were leaning in on her, making space only for her and the grief she hadn't unpacked.

She closed her eyes.

Inevitably, his name surfaced.

Alexei.

She didn't understand why he lingered in her thoughts. He was a stranger. A fleeting presence. But something about the way he had looked at her kept returning. It was the kind of gaze you didn't forget. It had weight. Intention. She didn't know what he saw in her that night, but she felt seen.

Then he was gone. No explanation. No note. Just an absence.

She'd tried to find him. Not seriously, at first. Just a casual search. Curiosity. She told herself it wasn't anything deeper, but there was nothing. No last name. No number. No online trace. Not even a mutual connection. It was as if he had never existed. Just Alexei, and the memory of his voice in her ear.

Love rolled onto her side, her hand settling on her chest. Beneath her fingers, her heartbeat felt slow and muffled.

Another memory bloomed.

Ophelia's graduation.

The air carried the scents of summer—fresh asphalt, cheap perfume, wildflowers blooming near the school fence. The gymnasium was packed, the lights too bright and unforgiving. Love had lingered near the back, her phone clutched tightly in her sweaty hands as her sister's name echoed across the room. The applause swelled, and there she was—Ophelia, bounding across the stage with her curls bouncing and a grin that seemed big enough to swallow the sun.

Despite the fights, the silences, the tension at home, Ophelia had pulled herself together. She walked that stage with a poise that belied the struggles they both knew. She had decided, just for this day, to let herself shine.

They ducked out early to avoid the crowd. Ophelia tugged her down the street to a small cafe with a peeling turquoise door. She ordered sparkling cider and made them split a slice of cake, laughing as she looped the gold tassel from her cap around her head like a crown. She looked absurd. She looked radiant.Love had laughed. She remembered laughing.

Somewhere between bites, Ophelia had looked up, wide-eyed and certain.

"We're going to make it," she said. "Together."

Love sat up abruptly. Her breath caught.

She clenched her fists, her nails pressing into her palms. That word kept echoing.

Together.

But now there was only her, in a room too full of silence and memories that wouldn't let go.

She reached into her coat and pulled out the folded page.

A car.

That was all she had...

But it would have to be enough.

◇ ◇ ◇ ◇ ◇ ◇ ◇ ◇ ◇

Chapter 6:

There You Are

The wind pushed hard against the windshield as Love navigated her sedan through the narrow streets of Acadia Falls. Beneath the flat gray sky, the town seemed even smaller, its twists and turns lined with familiar houses and weary storefronts. Time crawled in a place like this, where the first snow clung stubbornly until spring. Her tires crunched over frozen gravel as she eased into the lot of Acadia Auto, one of only two dealerships in town. The building, faded by decades of salt air and sun, had clearly once been modern—perhaps back when her parents were her age. Now it looked tired, almost forgotten.

The idea that a clue to her sister's murder might be buried here felt far-fetched; she was out of easy options.

Inside, the air was thick with the scents of rubber, oil, and too many cheap air fresheners. An older salesman approached from across the floor, his smile careful, his politeness just a little strained.

"Afternoon," he said, dragging out the word in a familiar Maine accent. "What can I do for you?"

Love didn't waste time. She pulled the folded police report from her coat pocket and held it in front of her. Her eyes dropped to the highlighted section, even though she already had the words memorized. Dark sedan. High-end. No license plate. Parked near the alley.

"I'm looking for a car," she said, her voice quieter than she intended. "Expensive. Black. Something that would stand out around here."

He raised an eyebrow, his smile faltering a little. "Could be anything. People come through here in all sorts of stuff when the weather's nice. BMWs, Lexuses. Seen a Tesla or two."

"Do you keep records?" she asked. "Sales, service appointments. Anything that might help."

He scratched his chin, glancing over his shoulder. "Sure, but it's not like we log them by color and vibe. Mostly move pickups and used SUVs. Still, I'll check."

He led her to a cluttered desk in the corner, where a dusty computer whirred to life with a loud hum. Love stood motionless, arms crossed tightly, her fingers digging into her sleeves as he clicked slowly through outdated software. The heater rattled behind her, blasting hot air that dried out her throat and left her skin itching.

He mumbled to himself as he scrolled. "Nope. Not that one. Wrong year. That's an old Ford..."

She waited a little longer, trying to stay hopeful, but her breath grew shallow. Her coat was starting to stick to her back from the heat, and the fake citrus smell of air fresheners made her stomach turn.

Without another word, she turned and walked out.

The next few hours blurred together. She visited another dealership, only to face another dead end. One man offered her coffee, another handed her a list of cars sold last fall, but none of the records matched what she was looking for. She scribbled barely legible notes in her notebook: makes, models, dates, guesses. Nothing seemed to fit. Hoping for a breakthrough, she stopped at a few small businesses near the alleyway to ask about security footage.

A manager handed her a flash drive with video from a camera facing the street. Her heart raced with cautious hope, but when she finally reviewed the footage on her laptop in the car, it proved almost entirely useless.

The angle was wrong, the timestamp flickered, and half the screen was blurred by glare. She stared at the grainy images anyway, like something might reveal itself if she just looked hard enough.

Nothing did.

By the time her phone rang, she was back at her car, fingertips red with cold. She answered without checking the screen.

"Any luck?" James asked. His voice was calm as ever, steady and familiar.

"Nothing," she said, pressing her forehead against the steering wheel. "I've been chasing shadows."

"Hey," he said, his voice softening. "We'll find something. Don't let it get to you."

"I'm not giving up," she replied, though she barely believed it herself. "It's just... exhausting. Every lead evaporates the second I reach for it."

"I'll poke around a little tonight," he said. "Some of those forums I checked might have chatter about something like this. You never know."

There was a pause. Something about the way he said it made her stomach twist. Lately, James's help had felt too convenient. He always seemed to know what she needed before she asked. She shook the thought away, swallowing it before it could take root.

"Thanks," she muttered, then ended the call.

❋ ❋ ❋ ❋

The snow had started again. Thin flakes floated through the air, softening the edges of the world. By the time she pulled into her driveway, her fingers ached and her shoulders felt like stone. The house looked just as it always did, dark windows and a quiet porch. She expected silence when she opened the door. Her mother stirring a pot on the stove, her father watching the news with the volume turned down.

Instead, there was laughter.

Love froze, one hand still gripping the doorknob, caught mid-motion as the sound filled the house. It wasn't cautious or soft; it rolled out from the kitchen, a low, resonant laugh that stopped her cold. Her mother's voice followed—high, bright, and unexpectedly light. The note of joy threaded through it made Love's stomach twist. She hadn't heard her mother sound that way since Ophelia.

Her bag slipped off her shoulder as her feet moved without thought. Her boots remained by the door, abandoned. Her pulse quickened with every step toward the kitchen, a rhythmic pounding that filled her ears. It wasn't fear exactly, though it made her chest feel tight. The closer she got, the more surreal it all became, as if she had stepped out of her own life and into something she couldn't quite name. Her hands trembled, but she kept moving, drawn forward by the sound of that laugh and the warmth in her mother's voice.

She stopped in the doorway.

There he was.

Standing at the counter, his back to her, tall and relaxed. His shoulders stretched broad under a dark sweater, his hair mimicking a shampoo commercial. He turned slightly, and the profile of his jaw struck her like a memory she didn't want to remember. A low laugh rolled out of him again, effortlessly rich and resonant, as though he had always been there. Her mother handed him a mug, smiling, as though this was the most normal thing in the world.

Love's throat tightened. Her legs felt heavy, her breath caught somewhere deep in her chest. She told herself it was anger, but she wasn't sure if that was entirely true. The sight of him there felt too raw, too close. It pushed at something she wasn't ready to acknowledge, a feeling she had tucked away, hidden even from herself.

Her mother saw her first, her face lighting up with a brightness Love barely recognized. "Love, there you are!" she called, as though nothing had shifted, as though this scene hadn't cracked the air around them.

He turned slowly at the sound of her name. There was no rush, no surprise. His movements were deliberate, his expression calm. He looked at her the way he always had—steady, unyielding, with that pale blue gaze that stripped away her defenses. She tried to summon anger, confusion, even indifference, but they tangled together into a knot that left her standing there, speechless.

The kitchen felt impossibly warm, the air too heavy. Her vision narrowed, the sound of her own pulse rising until it drowned out her mother's voice. She wanted to say something, to demand why he was here, to tell him to leave. Yet no words came, only the overwhelming sensation that her world had tilted and left her adrift.

They just stared at each other, frozen in a moment stretched too thin, like time had stepped back to watch.

Then, slowly, he smiled.

It was a polite smile, casual, maybe even kind, but it unsettled her more than if he had said something cruel. There was nothing overtly wrong about it—no smugness, no smirk, no malice—just a quiet curve of his mouth like this was perfectly normal, like this was how people ran into each other in kitchens all the time.

But there was nothing normal about this.

Love didn't smile back.

Her feet stayed planted, rooted in the floor as if her body didn't trust itself to move. Her lungs burned with the effort of holding herself still. Her mother spoke again, the words soft and welcoming, something about dinner and catching up, but Love still couldn't hear her.

All she could see was him.

Alexei, standing in her kitchen like the last time hadn't happened, like he hadn't vanished from her bed and her thoughts and left her wondering if any of it had even been real. Now he was here, laughing with her mother, comfortable, casual, close.

Chapter 7:

E ngineering Metaphors

The air in the kitchen thickened as if someone had turned up the humidity. Love's grip on the counter tightened. She hadn't realized how hard she was holding on until her knuckles burned. Across the room, Alexei stood leaning against her fridge, a picture of calculated ease. His charcoal shirt clung to his chest, dark denim hanging low on his hips, and those sharp blue eyes pinned her to the spot. It was the same Alexei, the same casual charm, the same unbearable confidence, but now, it felt different. Sharper. Like he knew something she didn't.

"Hey, Love," he said, his voice smooth, unbothered. "Nice place you've got here."

She stared at him, mouth dry, a thousand questions crashing into each other in her head. *How long has he been here? How did he even find me? Why does he look so... at home?* "Alexei," she finally managed, her voice coming out more hoarse than intended. "What—how—why are you here?"

He pushed away from the fridge with a lazy grace that sent her pulse into overdrive. His shoulders rolled back as he shrugged, that faint half-smile still hanging on his lips. "I wanted to see you," he said, like it was the most natural thing in the world. "You weren't here, so your mom said I could wait." He gave a short laugh, tilting his head toward the doorway. "By the way, she's quite the character."

Her heart pounded against her ribcage. "You talked to my mom?"

"Charming woman. Offered me tea. Said you'd be back soon." He crossed the kitchen, slow and deliberate, and stopped just a few feet away. "I figured I'd be patient."

Before she could respond, her mother's voice floated in from the dining room. "Love, darling, why didn't you tell us about this friend of yours?" Dahlia's cheerful tone set Love's teeth on edge. "Alexei's a delight."

Moments later, her mother appeared in the doorway, wiping her hands on her apron, a bright smile lighting up her face. She didn't seem at all fazed by Alexei's presence. On the contrary, she nudged him playfully with her elbow like they were old friends. Love felt her stomach drop.

"Imagine my surprise," Dahlia said with a laugh, "finding this young man here. And quite the looker, Love. You've been holding out on us."

Love opened her mouth, ready to explain or deny, but her words caught in her throat. She felt as though the strings holding her together had been cut, leaving her frozen and unsure.

"Alexei has been such a dear," her mother said, unaware of the turmoil inside her. "He helped me chop vegetables for the stew. He's quite the chef, too."

Love glanced at Alexei, who was already watching her. His smile remained steady, but his piercing blue eyes seemed to hold something unspoken. A challenge, perhaps, or some quiet understanding. Whatever it was, it pinned her in place, her breath suddenly shallow.

"Really. That's... unexpected," she said finally, forcing the words out. Her smile felt like a cheap mask. Her thoughts were too scattered to put together anything convincing. She couldn't understand why her mother was so at ease, why Alexei was even here, why this all felt so... rehearsed.

"Unexpected makes life interesting, don't you think?" Alexei's voice had that same subtle accent, a faint rhythm that always made his words sound deliberate. Intentional. Dangerous.

Dahlia chuckled, patting Alexei's arm as if he belonged here. "Oh, I agree. Love, sweetheart, why don't you get washed up for dinner? Alexei, you must stay. We'd love to have you."

"I'd be honored," Alexei replied, his tone dripping with charm. Love felt like she was watching a magician perform sleight of hand—distracting everyone while the real trick happened right in front of her.

The rest of the evening was no less surreal. Around the dining room table, Love's father, Ashton, sat at his usual place, carving the roast with the precision of a surgeon. His eyes darted toward Alexei every so often, sharp and calculating, as if he were analyzing a competitor in a game of chess.

"Alexei," Ashton said, setting down the carving knife, "I don't believe we've had the pleasure before. Chervyakov, was it? What do you do?"

Love's heart clenched. Her father's tone was as measured as his knife work—polite, yet edged. She glanced at Alexei, waiting for some crack in his perfect veneer. But Alexei didn't flinch.

"Engineering, sir," he said easily. "Structural engineering, to be exact."

"Engineering?" Ashton repeated, leaning back slightly. His hands rested on the table as he studied Alexei. "And what brings you to our corner of the world?"

Alexei smiled faintly, lifting his glass of wine. "Business. And Love, of course. I couldn't pass up the chance to see her again."

Love's chest tightened. The way he said her name made her feel like the center of a spotlight, but not the good kind. It was the kind that illuminated every flaw, every doubt, every fear. She looked down at her plate, wishing she could sink into the ground.

"Business," Ashton said, his tone neutral but his gaze cutting. "Real estate, I presume?"

"Real estate development," Alexei confirmed, matching Ashton's stare. "I find it rewarding. The challenge, the logistics... the opportunity to create something lasting."

The tension was palpable. Love saw her mother glance nervously between the two men, trying to smooth over the jagged edges. "Isn't that lovely," Dahlia interjected. "A man who builds things. That's admirable."

Love made herself eat, even though her appetite had vanished. Her father's deliberate questions, Alexei's carefully measured responses, and the staged feel of the entire dinner weighed on her. She couldn't concentrate, couldn't think clearly.

After dinner, she ended up gathering the plates with Alexei by her side. When his arm brushed against hers, it sent a jolt through her, sharp and electric. She looked up at him, and there it was again—that shadowed, knowing look she couldn't decipher.

"I owe you an explanation," he said softly. "I never meant to leave things the way I did."

She swallowed hard, her hands gripping the edge of the counter. "It was just one night," she said, her voice barely above a whisper. "Why now?"

"Because," he said, stepping closer, "I knew it wasn't just one night for you either."

His words were a direct hit, cutting through her defenses. She wanted to protest, to deny it, but the truth tangled in her throat. He leaned in slightly, close enough that she could feel his warmth, his presence enveloping her.

"I'm here now. I'll wait as long as you need," Alexei murmured, his thumb brushing lightly against her cheek.

Love stepped back just enough to break his touch, raising an eyebrow as if his words had no more weight than a weather report. "You always talk like you're in a movie, you know that?" she said, her tone dry. "What's next? A monologue about second chances?"

His mouth twitched at her remark, the faintest hint of a smirk tugging at his lips. "If that's what it takes."

She shook her head, folding her arms. "Do yourself a favor...stick to engineering metaphors. At least then you'll sound like a professional."

Alexei tilted his head slightly, as though studying her. "Point taken," he said, a glint of amusement in his eyes. "But I don't mind a challenge."

"Goodnight, Love," he added softly, pressing a kiss against her forehead.

He stepped back, a lingering warmth in the air, and turned to leave. The door clicked shut, the sound echoing in the sudden silence of the house. Love stood in the hallway, her fingers tracing the spot on her forehead where his lips had lingered. Why is he here? she thought, her mind a whirlwind of confusion and reluctant attraction. That night was good, but it was just one night. Is he always like this? What game is he playing? She couldn't shake the feeling that Alexei's sudden reappearance was more than just a chance encounter, and the enigma of his presence hung heavy in the air, leaving her with more questions than answers.

◈ ◈ ❧◈ ◈ ◈ ◈ ❧ ◈ ◈ ◈ ◈

Chapter 8:

Reformed Sinner

The decisive click of the front door latch echoed down the hallway like a gavel, final and unyielding. Love stood motionless, suspended between shock and spiraling thoughts, the ghost of Alexei's parting kiss still lingering on her skin. That forehead press—too soft for someone with such hard edges—burned like a brand now that he was gone. The air felt colder, quieter, as if the house itself had exhaled after holding its breath.

He'd walked in like he belonged—slipped into her kitchen, her mother's good graces, and then her nerves—without a hint of warning or apology. And now, just as easily, he'd disappeared back into the dusk, leaving only the unsettling ripple of his presence behind.

"Well!" Dahlia emerged from the dining room with a startling brightness, practically glowing. "Love, darling, who was that? Absolutely charming! And so handsome. My goodness, why have you been hiding such a distinguished friend?"

She nudged her daughter playfully, unaware of the inner chaos unraveling behind her daughter's wide eyes.

"Helped me with the stew, didn't even need asking. Said his name was Alexei. Is he new in town?"

Love's voice caught in her throat.

"Mom, I... he's... not exactly a friend," she said, her words landing with all the grace of a misstep on black ice.

She couldn't explain it—not the intimacy, not the ghosting, and certainly not the resurgence. The man who vanished after one night had just casually diced carrots with her mother like a reformed sinner.

Ashton stepped into the hallway, his arms folded, eyes narrowed with wary calculation. "He's smooth," he said bluntly. "Talks a good game. Engineering, real estate, international this and that. But did you notice? No real answers. No specifics about where he lives or what he's actually doing here."

He paused, dropping his voice. "How did he know where we lived, Love? Did you tell him?"

"No! Of course not," she snapped, heat rising in her face. "I barely know him."

That wasn't entirely true. She knew the slope of his jaw, the weight of his hands, the sound of his breath in a dark room. But that knowledge existed in a separate realm—one that had no place in this kitchen.

Ashton didn't press further, but the set of his jaw made it clear he didn't believe her entirely.

"I just need a minute," Love muttered, excusing herself before her parents could ask more. The house felt like it was closing in on her, the air heavy and the walls felt too close.

Upstairs, her room didn't feel like hers anymore. The soft lighting and warm blankets couldn't erase the chill crawling up her spine. She sat on the edge of the bed, every nerve humming with unease. Her laptop called to her like a weapon. She opened it, fingers flying across the keyboard.

Alexei Chervyakov.

Nothing. A few international records. Some academics. No social media, no local ties. Not even a LinkedIn profile. For a man in real estate and engineering, someone who should be visible in every corner of the internet, he was conspicuously absent.

She refined her search and added "Maine," added "Acadia Falls," added "construction permits." Still nothing. No press, no public contracts, no developer records. He wasn't just private. He was erased. Deliberately.

She closed the lid with a sharp click and leaned back. Ashton had called it. Something about Alexei was too smooth, too perfectly tailored. He wasn't just a ghost—he was a constructed fiction wrapped in real skin and designer wool.

Sleep came late and jagged, and when it did, it brought no rest. Love drifted through restless images—Ophelia's lifeless eyes, the dim alleyway, Alexei's smile bending into something darker, his silhouette bleeding into shadows.

She woke before sunrise, cold and rattled. The Maine sky outside her window was pale and accusing. Her sister's memory loomed large, pressing down on her chest with unrelenting grief. How could she entertain the idea of meeting this man when justice for Ophelia had yet to be found? Was she betraying her sister's memory for the thrill of mystery?

Her phone buzzed on the nightstand.

Unknown Number:

Morning, Love. Hope I didn't cause too much disruption last night. Your mother's stew was excellent. Still thinking about it. As promised, I'd like to take you for coffee when you have a moment this week. No pressure, just talk. Let me know. —Alexei

She stared at the screen. No apology. Just ease. Just calm.

Still thinking about stew?

You showed up at my family home uninvited and now we're reminiscing about soup?

The absurdity would've made her laugh if her skin wasn't crawling.

She needed perspective. She needed James.

Her fingers hovered, then pressed call.

"Love?" he answered quickly. "You okay?"

She barely let him finish. "You're not going to believe this."

She unfolded as she told him everything. The one-night stand, the ghosting, the reappearance, the dinner with her family, the casual text. She told him about the internet searches that led nowhere, about her father's wariness, about her own unease that didn't seem to settle even now.

James didn't interrupt much, just a quiet "What?" here, a "You're kidding" there.

When she finished, there was a long pause.

"Love... this guy's not normal. I don't know what his deal is, but people don't just materialize like that without an agenda. You need to be careful."

"I know," she whispered, feeling suddenly very tired.

He exhaled. "If you're meeting him, do it in public. Let me know where and when. And if he tries anything, anything, I want you to leave. No hesitation."

"I will."

After they hung up, she stared at Alexei's message again. Something in her gut told her this wasn't just about him. This was a thread—and if she pulled it hard enough, something buried might surface.

Maybe she wasn't chasing him at all.

Maybe she was chasing the truth.

With steady hands, she typed:

Coffee sounds okay. When were you thinking?

The reply came fast.

Tomorrow. 10 AM. The Raven's Perch Cafe downtown? My treat.

Love locked her phone and set it aside. The pieces were shifting. She didn't know what picture they formed yet but she'd find out. One way or another.

Chapter 9:

Skip The Motivational Speeches

The biting Maine wind clawed at Love's cheeks as she made her way toward The Raven's Perch Café, each gust slipping beneath her coat like cold fingers and whispering doubts she couldn't quiet. Her heartbeat matched her steps, quick and loud. She pulled her coat tighter, willing herself to stay composed. This wasn't a date. It was reconnaissance. A controlled pursuit of answers. She repeated it like a prayer, trying to drown out the tremor of anticipation beneath her ribs.

Choosing what to wear felt ridiculous and paralyzing. She'd discarded a dress—too eager. A hoodie—too casual. She'd settled on dark jeans, boots that made her feel grounded, and a soft, charcoal-grey sweater that clung to her in quiet defiance. Understated armor. When she caught her reflection in a shop window, the face that stared back looked too pale, eyes shadowed with exhaustion and unresolved grief. Her fingers brushed against the small silver locket resting against her collarbone. Inside, a photo of Ophelia smiled up at her—a fragment of the past she carried like a knife tucked just beneath the skin. This is for you, she thought. This is all for you.

Her phone buzzed in her pocket. James.

Heading to Raven's Perch now. 10 AM, she'd texted.

Okay. Public place is good. Be smart. Call me the second you leave. Keep your head clear, Love.

James was always steady, always grounding. His concern was familiar. Reassuring. But it also sharpened her awareness of the risk. She exhaled, her breath fogging in the frigid air, and pushed open the café door.

✧ ✧ ✧ ✧ ✧

Warmth enveloped her instantly. The Raven's Perch was all cinnamon air and coffee steam, windows clouded with condensation, and a low murmur of conversation that softened the sharp edges of her nerves. Inside, coats were draped over chairs, mugs clinked against saucers, and no one paid her any mind. A perfect place to blend in. A perfect place to disappear.

Then she saw him.

Alexei sat at a corner table near the back, just distant enough to watch the door, just close enough to appear casual. A black coffee sat untouched in front of him. He wasn't scrolling his phone or pretending to read. He was simply... waiting. Present. His navy sweater hugged his frame, the color echoing the sharp clarity of his eyes when they finally found hers.

A faint smile tugged at his lips, not triumphant, but certain. He rose smoothly as she approached, his height more striking than she remembered, his movements precise and composed.

"Love," he said, his voice low and velvet-lined, that faint Eastern European accent ghosting over every syllable. "You came."

She kept her face neutral. "You seemed very sure I would."

"I hoped," he said simply.

She slid into the chair across from him, placing her purse in the seat beside her, a subtle barrier she didn't need to explain. The waitress appeared, all cheerful oblivion, and Love ordered a black coffee; strong, simple, without room for sweetness.

Alexei watched her, the ghost of amusement flickering in his eyes. "Confidence," he said after the waitress left, "is essential. In business, of course. But also in life."

"Let's skip the motivational speeches," Love said flatly. "You showed up at my house without warning, charmed your way into my family's dinner, then disappeared again. You owe me explanations, not philosophy. Start with how you found me."

He didn't bristle. Instead, he steepled his fingers and regarded her with that maddening calm. "Fair," he murmured. "You deserve the truth. At least, what truth I can share."

He paused for a sip of coffee, as if preparing to testify.

"My work involves property development. Before a site is chosen, we run comprehensive assessments—zoning, infrastructure, community layout, historical usage. That means accessing tax records, sometimes old municipal registries. It's... deep digging."

She didn't interrupt. She let him continue, waiting for the catch.

"Your family name came up in relation to a parcel of land near a site I was reviewing. Not directly—it was adjacent, historically connected. But 'Love Godfrey' isn't the sort of name one forgets." He paused, his gaze steady. "I remembered the party. You. Confirmed the connection. And yes, I acted on impulse. I shouldn't have. But I had to see you again."

Love kept her expression unreadable. His explanation was neat. Too neat. Convenient. Detailed just enough to feel grounded in reality—but polished, curated. He could've been reciting from a script.

"And the disappearing act?" she pressed. "That morning. Why vanish without a word?"

His eyes dropped for a moment. When he looked back up, the gleam of charm was gone, replaced by something almost vulnerable. "There was a family emergency. Something I couldn't ignore. It pulled me out of state, out of reach. But... it's not an excuse. I should've left a note. I should've found a way to explain. I didn't. And I regret it."

Another smooth apology. Another carefully placed glimpse behind the curtain. And yet, it didn't ring false. Just incomplete.

Their drinks arrived. Love took a sip, needing the bitterness to focus. Alexei shifted, his posture softening as he leaned forward slightly.

"Your mother mentioned journalism. Communications. Tell me, what drew you to that world?"

Love hesitated. She didn't want to offer pieces of herself. But she also didn't want to seem afraid. So she gave him a version of the truth.

"Stories matter. Truth matters. Someone has to speak when no one else will."

He nodded, as if the answer pleased him. "That's rare," he said. "And dangerous, sometimes. Truth is a blade, isn't it?"

"If you're scared of being cut," she replied, "you're probably hiding something."

Alexei let out a low chuckle. "Touché."

She redirected. "You mentioned travel. Work. Family. You seem to move a lot."

He shrugged slightly. "My father's family is Russian. I've spent time in Moscow, St. Petersburg. My work takes me where it needs to. As for family... we're complicated. I have a half brother. Estranged. Different paths. Different rules."

He gave no names. No specific roles. Just shadows in place of people.

"And the work you're doing here?" she asked. "What kind of development?"

"Mixed-use commercial," he replied smoothly. "Retail offices. Sustainability-focused. But it's early. Mostly research and feasibility. Legal constraints mean I can't say much more."

She filed away every vague term, every elegant dodge. He was good. But not perfect.

Still, he had an unnerving gravity to him, something that pulled at her, despite every alarm in her body. There was a moment when his hand brushed hers—accidental, surely—and she felt her pulse spike, unwanted but undeniable.

When a toddler at a nearby table let out a triumphant shout about syrup, both of them glanced over at the same time. Love laughed unexpectedly, and Alexei's smile deepened as if he'd just won a round without playing.

He glanced at his watch; sleek, expensive, understated. "I've overstayed, haven't I?" he said, a rare note of hesitation slipping into his tone. "I have a call to prepare for. Unfortunately."

He didn't move right away. Instead, he reached for his coat slowly, brushing nonexistent creases from the sleeves, his gaze lingering on her with a quiet deliberateness that made the seconds stretch. For a man who had sidestepped half her questions and cloaked himself in calculated mystery, his silence now felt strangely unguarded.

"It meant something to see you again," he said, voice low and even, with none of the polished charm he'd worn like armor earlier. "Even if I can't explain why. Not yet."

Love looked up at him, unsure what to say. The room felt warmer suddenly, not from comfort, but from proximity to something she couldn't name.

"I'll be around for a few more days," he added, slipping his coat on with practiced ease. "Still tying up a few things here." He paused, then tilted his head.

"If you find yourself wanting more answers... or just good coffee... I won't be far."

He gave a nod that felt more like a question abandoned mid-thought, then turned toward the door. His steps carried no urgency and no grandeur, only the slow erosion of presence. One moment, he was there. The next, he was unraveling, slipping from her world with the quiet certainty of a stone sinking out of sight. His absence left the room stretched thin, like a silence pulled too tight to hold.

Love sat still, fingers curled loosely around her coffee cup, the steam long since vanished. She didn't watch the door, didn't let herself. But something in her pulse remained off-kilter.

He'd given her more than she expected and less than she needed.

She didn't trust him...but she wasn't finished with him, either.

◇◇ ◇ ❧ ◇ ◇◇ ◇ ❧ ◇

Chapter 10:

Houdini-level Ghosting

The artificial hum of the Channel 5 newsroom buzzed behind Love like a fluorescent migraine. Her desk, usually a cluttered battleground of coffee cups and half-finished drafts, now looked more like a crime scene — images from Ophelia's file spread across the surface, interspersed with scribbled interview notes and municipal records. The weight of it pressed down on her chest like wet wool. And weaving through it all, like a fine thread stitched into every corner of her consciousness, was Alexei Chervyakov. His smooth voice. That carefully curated mystery. The message from James—Play it cool, observe him more, see what slips—was on loop in her brain, except nothing about him ever slipped. It all felt too neat.

Her phone buzzed, a flash of Layla's name on the screen. Love stared at it for a beat before answering.

"Love Godfrey," Layla began with theatrical exasperation, "you have some serious explaining to do. And don't bother trying to lie! I've already been briefed by James. I can't believe you didn't tell me your mystery man waltzed into your mother's kitchen."

Love closed her eyes, dragging her hand down her face. "Layla, I—"

"No, don't start with the whole 'I was going to tell you' routine. You've been Houdini-level ghosting me for weeks."

Guilt coiled in her gut. "You're right," she admitted. "I've been... overwhelmed. With everything."

There was a pause.

Then, Layla's tone softened—just slightly.

"I get it. I do. But if you're going to go dark, you don't get to leave me out when the plot gets juicy. Lucky for you, I've decided on a path to redemption. You,me, James. This weekend. My cousin's cabin up by Moosehead Lake—secluded, snowy, no internet, perfect for guilt trips and emotional resets."

Love blinked. "That sounds like a very elaborate trap."

"Oh, it is. But also, it's happening. I already invited James. And if you really want forgiveness," Layla continued, her voice sly now, "bring Alexei."

Love sat back. "Are you serious?"

"I'm deadly serious," Layla said. "We get to meet him. James gets to psychoanalyze him. You get plausible deniability for continuing this... situation. Everyone wins. Unless, of course, you want me to remain mad at you and uninformed."

Love hesitated. It was reckless. But she remembered James's words: Let him think he's winning you over. Let the act slip.If Layla and James were both there, maybe Alexei would reveal something new—something real.

"Fine," she said at last. "But you're buying the marshmallows."

ALEXEI'S RESPONSE CAME almost too quickly:

Love, that sounds like exactly what I need. A welcome break. Count me in.

She texted James next:

Layla roped us into a weekend at her cousin's cabin. Friday to Sunday. She insisted I invite Alexei. He's coming.

James's reply was less enthusiastic:

Okay. I'll keep my eyes open. Just... don't let charm fog the mission. Trust your gut.

✦ ❧❧ ✦ ❧❧ ✦ ❧

The road to Moosehead Lake was a winding ribbon of snow-slick asphalt flanked by endless pine. By the time they reached the cabin, dusk had fallen in watercolor streaks of purple and slate. The pine-scented air was sharp, untouched by city static. As James pulled into the gravel drive, Layla's Subaru was already there, and moments later, Alexei's SUV glided in with all the ease and grace its driver possessed.

He stepped out dressed for the cover of a winter fashion catalog—wool coat, leather gloves, effortlessly tousled hair. He greeted them with a faint smile, the kind that implied he'd expected to be there all along.

Inside, the cabin pulsed with firelight and Layla's relentless energy. "Welcome to snowy isolation!" she cheered. "Where board games, gossip, and mild psychological warfare await!"

Alexei offered her a vacuum-sealed bag of expensive coffee beans and a wedge of artisanal cheese. "Provisions for survival," he said, then handed a bottle of single malt to James with a nod. "And peace offerings."

James accepted it with a quiet "Thanks," and they shared a brief handshake. Something passed in that moment—a flicker behind Alexei's eyes. Curiosity? Recognition? But he said nothing.

Love felt caught in the crosscurrents, acutely aware of the dynamics at play. The sheer exhaustion from the drive and the underlying stress finally hit her hard. While the others were debating the merits of scotch versus hot chocolate for the first evening, she felt an overwhelming need to retreat.

"Hey guys," she said, managing a tired smile. "I think that drive knocked me out more than I realized. I'm just going to drop my stuff in my room and maybe splash some water on my face. Be back in a bit."

"No problem!" Layla called out. "Take five! We'll hold down the fort!"

Love escaped to the small, cozy bedroom assigned to her. The sudden quiet was a relief. She dropped her bag, the silence amplifying the faint ringing in her ears. Just sitting on the edge of the simple pine bed felt like a monumental act of surrender. She closed her eyes, just for a moment, letting the stillness wash over her... and exhaustion claimed her instantly.

◇ ☙ ◇ ☙ ◇

A soft tapping on her door roused Love. Sunlight, intensely bright against the snow outside, spilled across the wooden floor in long golden lines. She blinked, momentarily disoriented, then realized with a jolt that she'd slept through the entire evening and night, still fully clothed, her boots still at an odd angle by the side of the bed.

"Love?" Layla's voice came muffled through the door. "I come bearing bribes."

Love groaned softly, rubbing her eyes. When she opened the door, Layla stood there holding two mismatched mugs of coffee, looking smugly victorious.

Beside her was Alexei, hair damp from the morning air, his own mug cradled loosely in one hand.

"We almost sent James to dig you out," he said smoothly, eyes glinting with amusement. "But he was sharpening a stick for a makeshift sled, and that felt... aggressive."

Love took the mug from Layla, its warmth seeping gratefully into her hands. "Thanks," she mumbled. "I'm still about 40% dreams and 60% blanket right now, so you may regret waking me."

Layla breezed past her into the room. "Ten minutes," she said over her shoulder. "We're hiking. And Alexei promised to show us how to tell the difference between bear tracks and moose."

Alexei raised an eyebrow, deadpan. "I said nothing of the sort. I said moose are larger and more terrifying. That was the extent of my wildlife expertise."

Love shook her head and turned back toward the small en suite bathroom. "Ten minutes," she called. "But if I come back and someone's eaten all the trail mix, I'm pushing you into the lake."

"Bold of you to assume I wouldn't float," Layla called back.

The hike, to Love's surprise, turned out to be exactly what she needed. The sky was a brilliant, cloudless blue, and the snow sparkled like crushed diamonds underfoot. The trail wound gently around the lake and through a quiet patch of evergreens, their dark green boughs dusted with frost.

Laughter threaded through the trees, loose and wild, catching in the bare branches like a memory too stubborn to fade. Layla cursed her "waterproof" boots with every splash, her voice cutting through the cold in bursts of color. James kept pace beside them, muttering half-hearted warnings about hidden patches of ice while steadying anyone who stumbled.

Alexei stayed a few steps back, not leading, not lingering, just present in a way that filled the silence without needing to break it. He pointed out a hawk circling overhead, the glint of frost along a fallen log, the soft tremor of ice about to give underfoot. When Love slipped, her balance faltering for the briefest second, his hand found hers without hesitation. His fingers closed around her wrist, firm and careful, and when she looked up, his half-smile met her like a secret the world was not meant to see.

At some point, James and Alexei drifted ahead, their voices lowered to a register she couldn't catch. Layla slipped her arm through Love's and leaned in, her presence warm and conspiratorial.

"Okay," she whispered. "Mystery man's hot. But he gives me 'definitely owns a private vault' vibes. Probably keeps a rare violin and a list of his enemies in there."

Love snorted. "You have no idea. You should've seen him explain zoning regulations over coffee. I felt like I was being seduced and audited at the same time."

Layla cackled. "That's a man who's either got deep emotional trauma or a second identity. Possibly both."

"Don't forget the expensive cologne and an accent that shifts slightly depending on who he's talking to," Love added dryly.

"Mm. Sexy red flag behavior. If I weren't already emotionally bankrupt, I'd flirt just to stir the pot."

Love bumped her shoulder against Layla's. "Thanks for making me come."

"You needed it," Layla said, her voice softening. "And... for what it's worth, I'm glad he's here. Watching him helps me know if he's worth the slow burn obsession you're clearly trying to repress."

"I'm not obsessed," Love said quickly. Then: "...Just mildly... perplexed."

"Sure," Layla said, giving her a look. "And I'm the Virgin Mary."

They continued on in easy silence, the only sound of their boots in the snow and the rustle of wind through the trees. When they reached a clearing near the ridge overlooking the lake, James tossed down a blanket from his pack, and they sat for a while, passing around chocolate bars and flasks of coffee, letting the stillness settle.

Alexei sat beside Love, close enough that their shoulders brushed. He didn't say much, just occasionally glanced over with an unreadable expression, like he was trying to memorize her profile.

Eventually, James stood and stretched. "We should head back before the temperature drops."

Layla let out a dramatic groan. "Back to civilization? No thanks. Let me freeze in the woods. I'll become one with nature."

"You won't even walk barefoot on your balcony," Love muttered.

"Exactly," Layla said. "It'll be poetic."

They made their way down the trail as the sky began to shift—pale blue giving way to amber-gold, the light turning softer, richer, as if warming the trees one last time before night settled in.

By the time they returned to the cabin, the hearth had been lit, the windows were aglow, and the scent of dinner (mostly Layla reheating frozen lasagna and calling it 'rustic') filled the air.

The silence did not settle; it expanded, filling the spaces between heartbeats.

✧ ✧ ✧ ✧ ✧

That evening, after dinner, the fire burned low. Layla had collapsed on the couch with a half-eaten bag of popcorn, and James disappeared into the guest room claiming early hiking plans. That left her and Alexei alone, the flicker of flames casting gold against the cabin's stone walls.

Love stood near the wide window, arms crossed tightly over her chest. The glass had fogged slightly from the warmth of the room meeting the cold night beyond, blurring the outline of snow-draped pines outside. Her reflection wavered faintly, and in it, she saw him approach before she heard him.

"You think too loudly," Alexei said, voice low, almost amused.

She didn't turn. "You eavesdrop too silently."

A quiet hum of a chuckle, not quite laughter. "Occupational hazard."

They stood like that for a beat—two silhouettes reflected in glass, surrounded by firelight and shadows. The silence between them wasn't awkward. It was charged. Cautious. Curious.

"You wear your grief like armor," he said finally, more observation than judgment.

That made her turn. Her brow arched, slow and sharp. "And what would you know about grief?"

He didn't answer right away. Instead, he swirled the amber liquid in his glass, watching it catch the firelight.

"My father believed suffering was necessary. That pain carved character. He thought endurance was the ultimate measure of a man." A pause, soft but weighted. "He taught me to bury things so deep they stopped feeling real."

Love watched him carefully now, all pretense of banter slipping between them like melting snow. There was something in his voice—quiet, precise, but edged with something rawer. A crack in the surface. No velvet accent, no curated mystique. Just... a man. Haunted. Tired.

"I don't talk about him," he said. "But tonight, standing here, I thought maybe... maybe you'd understand."

His gaze didn't seek hers for validation. He wasn't looking to be comforted. He was simply offering the truth—one fragile piece of it—like something he might take back if touched too roughly.

She didn't offer sympathy. Didn't reach out.

But she didn't move away either.

The fire crackled gently in the hearth behind them. A log split with a sharp pop. The sound made them both flinch.

Alexei took a sip of his drink, then set the glass down on the narrow ledge near the window. "I should get some rest," he said, and just like that, the door began to close again. His tone had shifted—cooler, more distant, as if whatever had opened had been enough for now.

Still, he lingered.

"Tomorrow," he added quietly, not looking at her this time, "if you want to talk... I'll follow your lead."

There was no pressure in it. No expectation. Just space—offered, not demanded.

Love nodded, just once. "Goodnight, Alexei."

He turned to go but paused in the threshold, half in shadow, half caught in the amber glow of the fire. "Goodnight, Love," he said, and this time, her name wasn't a plaything on his tongue. It was a soft imprint.

After he disappeared down the hallway, she remained rooted by the window, the quiet settling in again like dust. His words stayed with her—not just the content of them, but the way he said them. Like someone who didn't tell stories easily, and certainly not to be understood. But tonight, maybe... he wanted to be seen.

Alexei was still a mystery. But not the cartoon villain she'd tried to make him out to be. No, something worse.

He wasn't a monster.

He was a man.

And that, perhaps, was far more dangerous. Because monsters, you could name. You could run from them.

But people like Alexei?
They made you hesitate.
And hesitation was the first step toward losing yourself.

Chapter 11:

Emotions Are A Liability

Sunday morning arrived in a haze of white and gold. The cabin was cocooned beneath a thick quilt of snow, every branch outside draped in crystalline frost that glittered under a cloudless sky. It was the kind of winter morning that almost dared you not to feel hope.

Inside, the air was filled with the scent of coffee and the sounds of Layla humming off-key as she flipped pancakes in mismatched socks. The world outside had slowed, quieted, and the sense of stillness seeped into Love's bones in a way she hadn't realized she needed.

They lingered over breakfast, their conversation meandering through silly topics—bad childhood haircuts, worst celebrity baby names, whether James had ever owned a fedora (he had, and regretted it)—until Layla, unable to contain herself a moment longer, leapt from her chair and declared, "Enough serenity! We are engaging in combat. Last chance for snowball war glory, people. Loser scrubs the kitchen floor."

"Are you twelve?" James asked mildly, already pushing back his chair.

"Only in the ways that matter," she shot back with a wink, sprinting toward the door.

What followed was glorious mayhem. Snow flew like powdered chaos. Love shrieked when a perfectly compacted snowball hit her square between the shoulders, only to spot Alexei behind a tree, his grin wide and unapologetic, eyes gleaming with challenge. He looked like a man unburdened by shadow—laughing, breath fogging in the cold, snowflakes caught in his hair.

It was disarming.

She retaliated, ducked a blow from James, and before she could stop herself, laughter broke free—sharp and breathless, tearing through the cold. Her sides ached, her cheeks flushed, and for a brief, reckless moment, the weight she carried dissolved into the air around her. Alexei's smile, so often a weapon or a shield, softened as he lobbed a snowball wide, missing her on purpose.

Eventually, wet and breathless, they trudged back inside. The cabin was warm with woodsmoke and soft light, the kind of light that invited easy conversation and contented silence. While Layla made cocoa and James tended the fire, Alexei helped Love wring out her gloves by the sink.

"You have a good arm," he said, deadpan.

"You have a good aim," she countered, suspiciously.

"Only when it counts."

The rest of the afternoon passed in a gentle blur; packing, laughing, Layla insisting on group photos. There was a rhythm to it all that felt... almost normal. Almost real.

When it came time to leave, they stood on the porch, the snow crunching underfoot, suitcases at their feet. Layla hugged Love like she meant it, whispering, "We'll unpack later. Everything." Then to Alexei: "You're alright. Annoyingly mysterious, but alright."

Alexei offered James a polite nod, which was returned in kind. There was none of yesterday's strange tension, just two men politely acknowledging each other. Whatever that flicker had been, it was either buried or tabled.

As when Love turned to walk toward James's car, Alexei caught her hand lightly.

"Thank you," he said, his voice pitched low, meant only for her. "For the invitation. This weekend was... more than I expected."

There was a quiet sincerity in his voice, something raw that caught her off guard and pressed against a part of her she hadn't let feel in a while. He paused before speaking again. "The offer still stands. Dinner. When you're ready."

She nodded, unsure what to say. He squeezed her hand once, gently, and then walked toward his SUV without another word.

◇ ◇ ◇ ◇

The quiet stretched as they drove south, trees blurring past in snowy halos. Love watched the landscape shift from wild to suburban, and the deeper they went, the more the weekend felt like something imagined.

"He fits in easily," James said at last, not quite a judgment.

Love rested her head against the cold window, eyes tracking the skeletal trees lining the highway. "He's hard to pin down," she said, not looking at him. "Like he's both exactly what he says he is... and something else entirely."

James hummed in agreement. "Just don't forget why you're looking."

The days that followed unraveled quickly—school, internship, a stack of neglected readings. She threw herself into it all with sharp precision, trying not to think about how easily Alexei had slipped into her orbit, but it wasn't working.

On Wednesday, a quiet detour on her way back from a courthouse errand led her through a quieter downtown street—full of law offices, private financial firms, quiet plaques for companies with names no one ever spoke aloud. That's where she saw it. A dark grey SUV, clean and expensive, parked between two black sedans. It might've been nothing. But her gut disagreed.

She kept walking.

Thursday came with a message:

Hope your week is manageable. Passed that little bookstore near the harbor, the one you mentioned. Thought of you.

She read it twice before replying simply:

Appreciate the thought. Hope your week's better than the coffee I'm currently drinking.

Friday arrived with another:

One more gamble. Dinner tonight? No pressure. Just good food and a quiet place to think.

She stared at her screen for a long time before answering.

Okay. Dinner tonight.

The restaurant he chose, The Mariner's Table, sat just off the harbor, tucked behind a row of artisan shops and nautical bookstores. It was all polished wood and low jazz and soft shadows. The kind of place that knew how to stay discreet.

Alexei was already waiting when she arrived, suit sharp but open-collared, a coat draped behind him. He stood when he saw her, and she swore his expression changed. She felt the shift in the air.

"You look..." he paused, eyes catching the green silk of her blouse, "unreasonably stunning."

"You look like you planned that line all day," she replied, dry.

"I did," he said, unbothered. "And it was worth it."

They sat. Before she could say more, he pulled out a small, wrapped parcel. "Not flowers," he said, sliding it across the table. "Too predictable."

Inside was an antique map of the Maine coastline, stunning in its detail, its ink faded but still elegant.

"It's beautiful," she said softly. "You didn't have to..."

"I wanted to," he interrupted, voice softer now. "I thought... maybe it would mean something."

And it did. More than she could admit.

He spoke more freely now. Maybe it was the wine, or the quiet pull of the moment.

"My father worships control. Timelines. Measurable outcomes. He thinks life is a ledger. Balanced when you're ruthless, efficient. Emotion, to him, is... a liability."

He exhaled slowly, his thumb absently brushing the rim of his glass.

"My mother was chaos in a linen dress. Loud opinions, soft hands. She made everything feel like a Sunday morning. She laughed with her whole body—God, she laughed at everything."

A faint, flickering smile ghosted his lips before vanishing.

"She died in an airport terminal."

Love's breath caught.

"Delayed layover in Amsterdam. She wandered off while waiting for her connecting flight. No calls. No signs. They found her slumped on a bench near Gate 14, book still open in her lap. Brain aneurysm. Instant."

He looked down, lashes low.

"No warning. No pain, they said. Just gone. One moment, the world had color. The next, it didn't."

Love said nothing. There wasn't a right thing to say.

Alexei didn't seem to need words, just silence that didn't ask anything of him.

He let out a quiet laugh...hollow, careful.

"My father didn't even attend her funeral. Said grief was 'a distraction.' I was nineteen. I planned it myself."

He met her eyes again, and this time there was no mask. Just devastation, held tightly under polished glass.

"I think the worst part isn't that she died. It's how the world didn't stop. It just... kept going. Like she hadn't been the axis."

He paused, the silence stretching—not uncomfortable, but weighted. Then, quieter:

"I know... hearing all this—the mother who died too suddenly and the father who's basically a Russian Gordon Gekko—probably sends a red flag flapping in your head."

A humorless curve pulled at his mouth. "Maybe you're wondering if I'm wired the same way. If I'm just like him."

His thumb tapped once against the table.

"Some people become their trauma. Some... spend their whole lives trying to be anything but."

Love didn't speak at first. Her fingers traced the rim of her water glass, her thoughts catching up to the weight of what he'd just offered. It wasn't vulnerability for vulnerability's sake. It was measured. Intentional. But real, all the same.

"I think... most people become a little bit of both," she said finally, her voice low but steady. "You don't always get to choose how the damage shows up. Sometimes it's not about what you're trying to be—it's about what you're trying not to become. And the harder you fight it, the more it leaks out sideways."

She glanced up, met his gaze. "You seem like someone who learned to survive by keeping things neat. Controlled. Polished. But that kind of survival comes at a cost, doesn't it?"

Her mouth tugged into something between a smile and a sigh. "For what it's worth, I don't think you're your father. But I also don't think you're immune to him, either."

Alexei stayed quiet. He watched her, steady and unflinching, the way someone might watch a storm they knew they could not outrun. He didn't try to fill the silence with reassurances or apologies. He simply stayed, a presence weighted with all the things he wasn't saying.

Love leaned back, her hand brushing the edge of the old map he had given her. The parchment was delicate under her fingertips, the lines of ink worn thin with time. She traced them absently, wondering if he had chosen it himself, or if it had been curated for him like so much of his life seemed to be.

The plates had been cleared. Their coffee had gone cold. Around them, the restaurant hummed with soft conversations and the clink of silverware, a low, numbing background that barely touched the moment stretching between them.

It should have felt ordinary. Nothing about it did.

She lifted her eyes to him again, finding him still watching, silent, composed. There was no demand in it. No expectation. Just a quiet endurance, like he had already accepted whatever ending waited at the edge of this night.

Love reached for her coat, the motion heavier than she intended. She smoothed her palm across the worn fabric of the map once more before letting it go.

Outside, the snow had stopped. The air was crisp and still, the kind that made your breath feel sharp in your lungs. The glow from the antique streetlamp cast shadows across the cobblestones as they approached her car, neither rushing the moment.

"Thank you for tonight, Love," Alexei said. His voice had dropped into something lower—sincere, almost reverent. "For trusting me enough to come. For giving this... whatever this is... a second breath."

"Thank you for dinner," she replied, voice quiet, unsure. "And for the map. It was unexpected. And oddly perfect."

He moved closer, not like a threat, but like something inevitable. The heat of him brushed against her skin before his hand even found her. His fingers traced the curve of her jaw, slow and weightless, as if memorizing the shape of a decision he had not yet made.

"There's so much more beneath the surface," he murmured. "For both of us."

His eyes captured her, holding her in a silence thick enough to bruise. She felt her breath catch, her instincts faltering between fear and something deeper, something unnamable. She braced herself for a kiss, unsure if she was ready or already ruined.

He moved closer with a gravity that made her chest tighten. When he kissed her temple, it was careful, almost solemn, the kind of touch that did not demand anything but left everything broken in its wake.

The moment clung to her skin, to her pulse, a quiet undoing she would not escape. He pulled back without a word, and for one aching heartbeat, she thought she could still feel the imprint of him, stitched into her bones like a secret too sacred to name.

She stood motionless, caught between the life she had built and the one he had just shattered open without ever asking.

When he pulled back, his hand still lingered near her cheek. "May I call you?"

"You already know the answer," she said, her voice barely audible.

He smiled, but it was smaller now. Sadder. "Goodnight, Love."

He walked away, his steps heavier than usual, as if every inch between them came with a cost he wasn't ready to name. Love didn't move. She remained there, rooted in the space he left behind, eyes fixed on the door that closed without ceremony. Her fingers lifted to her temple, desperately searching for a center that no longer existed. The air around her felt unfamiliar. Not cold, not warm. Just strange. Like grief pretending to be calm.

Something inside her shifted. Quietly. Fatally

◈ ◈ ✦ ◈ ◈ ◈ ◈ ✦ ◈ ◈

Chapter 12:

Lyubov Moya (My Love)

The Saturday after the cabin weekend felt like waking up inside someone else's skin. Love lay in bed long after the sun rose, her eyes fixed on the ceiling as strips of winter light filtered through the blinds and cut across her comforter in pale, surgical lines. The house was quiet. Too quiet. The kind of quiet that didn't soothe, but accused. Like the world had moved on without telling her.

Everything inside her felt suspended, caught in some strange in-between. She kept replaying it all in her head—Layla's laughter echoing through snow-covered trees, the flicker of James's shadow near the firepit, and that unbearable heat in Alexei's eyes. She remembered the moment his voice lowered when he spoke about his father, that almost imperceptible drop that felt like confession, like she was hearing something she wasn't supposed to.

There were too many threads now. All tangled. All layered in ways she hadn't accounted for.

By noon, she forced herself out of bed and onto the floor of her bedroom, where Ophelia's case files lay waiting in a haphazard circle around her desk. She sat cross-legged in the center, surrounded by memories that didn't belong to her. Pages curled at the edges, scrawled post-its in different colors, photocopied reports that reeked faintly of mildew and printer toner. She shuffled through them blindly, not looking for anything in particular, just hoping the rhythm of touching paper might pull her brain back into focus.

Her eyes skimmed over the details without absorbing them.

Instead, her fingers drifted to the margins. She began to sketch.

It wasn't intentional. She didn't even realize what she was doing until she looked down and saw the shape of a face. Angular. Closed. A familiar shadow forming where it shouldn't have.

Alexei.

She recognized the slant of his jaw. The curve of his lower lip. The dark hollows where his eyes should have been.

She stared at the drawing for a long moment, then scratched through it until the page tore.

This was never meant to be about him. Yet somehow, he found his way in. Not in grand, sweeping gestures, but slowly, steadily, like mist seeping through unseen cracks, until he was everywhere she tried not to look.

Right on cue, her phone rang.

His name lit up the screen.

She answered before her rational mind had time to interfere.

"Love," he said, and the sound of his voice was warm enough to hurt. "Just checking in. How's your day going?"

She hesitated, then admitted, "Trying to focus on work. Not really succeeding."

A soft chuckle hummed through the speaker. "In that case, I have a proposition. How do you feel about homemade Beef Stroganoff? Family recipe. Mildly legendary. Unless you've sworn off Russian comfort food."

His voice dipped at the edges of the joke, turning something light into something weighty.

Dinner. At her place.

A new line was being drawn in the sand, and she could feel it in her bones. She should've said no. Should've asked why he wanted to cook in her kitchen. Why now? But it didn't feel like a trap. It felt like a test.

Or maybe a door.

"Tuesday?" she said.

He paused. "Tuesday it is."

◇ ◇ ◇ ◇ ✦ ◇

When Tuesday arrived, she spent the afternoon reorganizing her spice rack with the kind of obsessive focus usually reserved for crime scene reconstructions. Her parents were out for the evening, a theatre show across town that would keep them occupied well into the night. The house was hers, though it didn't feel like it.

It felt... staged. Off. Like a replica of home that had been reassembled by someone who hadn't lived there.

She lit a candle. Then blew it out. Then lit it again.

She told herself this wasn't a date. She repeated that it was about observation, strategy, control. But then she changed her sweater twice and reapplied her lip balm three times and the lie started to taste familiar.

When he arrived, he brought a bottle of wine and a canvas tote filled with fresh groceries. He looked like he belonged in every room he entered, like no environment could reject him. She wondered if that was a skill he'd learned—or something that came with the name.

"You weren't joking," she said, stepping aside as he entered.

"I never joke about food," he replied, setting the bag on the counter. "And besides, you looked like you needed something warm."

She didn't know what to say to that. It shouldn't have landed the way it did.

Cooking together turned out to be more intimate than she anticipated. He moved like he already knew the depths of her kitchen, reaching for pans and utensils without hesitation. The scent of garlic and onions filled the air, layered over with something creamier. She stood beside him, unsure of what to do with her hands, caught between distraction and suspicion.

"Try this," he said, offering her a spoonful of the sauce.

She tasted it. It was perfect. Silky. Deep. Comforting in a way that almost made her uncomfortable.

When she looked up, he was already watching her.

Then his phone buzzed.

She watched the shift in real time. He didn't make a sound, didn't sigh or frown, but something in his spine straightened, his eyes narrowing a fraction before he glanced down.

He murmured something under his breath. Russian. "Proshu Proshcheniya."(I'm sorry).

Then he stepped outside to take the call.

She didn't follow. But she listened. Not for the words as she didn't speak the language, but the tone. The cadence. The way his voice clipped into commands, sharper than anything she'd heard from him before.

By the time he returned, his smile was intact, but it sat on his face like a coat worn inside out. He poured the wine, made small talk, but the warmth from earlier had cooled.

Dinner was still good. But something had shifted.

It didn't come back.

Not until they stood beside each other rinsing dishes, sleeves damp, fingers brushing when they reached for the same plate. He tucked a piece of hair behind her ear.

"Despite the interruption," he said softly, "I enjoyed this."

She nodded. "Me too."

He turned to her slowly, his hands lifting as though drawn by a force older than instinct. His palms cradled her face, thumbs brushing beneath her eyes where exhaustion had settled like dust. He studied her with quiet reverence, as if memorizing every fracture in her resolve before it gave way completely.

Love's body held its ground, not rigid but still. Her breath stilled in her chest, caught between fight and surrender. Logic whispered to run, to close off, to return to the safer kind of silence—but her feet didn't move. Her ribs stayed open.

When his lips met hers, it wasn't hunger that led him. It was something quieter. Something sacred. He kissed her like a prayer spoken in a language only they understood, like the weight of everything they'd lost could be eased, just for a moment, in this impossible proximity.

She didn't resist. She didn't want to. Not here. Not now. Not in this space carved from shared ache and unsaid things.

They undressed each other slowly, not with haste or greed, but with reverence. His hands traced her skin like scripture, memorizing, worshipping. Her fingers slipped through the buttons of his shirt as if learning him all over again, not to conquer, but to understand. He looked at her like she was a threshold. She touched him like he might disappear if she blinked too hard.

There were no sharp edges. No need for words. Only breath and the sound of fabric falling, the hush of skin finding skin. The air shifted, not into heat, but into gravity. The kind that holds everything down, that pulls truths out of hiding.

When his mouth brushed her shoulder, she closed her eyes. He kissed her like he was translating her pain. She trembled, not from fear, but from the unbearable relief of being seen.

This was not lust. This was vulnerability in its rawest form. It was trust in borrowed time. It was grief holding grief, touch learning touch, ruin recognizing ruin.

He moved over her with quiet purpose, fitting into the space between her legs as though he had always been meant to. Their eyes met, holding a conversation too sacred for sound. Then he entered her—slowly, deliberately—and her gasp cracked through the silence like something ancient being exhaled. Her back arched, her fingers curled, and her body answered his like a song half-remembered.

Their rhythm was wild, driven by need and memory and the kind of hunger that only heartbreak can grow. They didn't speak. Didn't whisper promises. Their mouths met, their bodies found their cadence, and the world outside vanished. Every thrust broke something. Every kiss stitched it closed.

He moved like he was trying to memorize the shape of her grief. She held onto him like she didn't trust the air to catch her if she let go. Sweat collected between their bodies. His mouth trailed over her jaw, her collarbone, the soft bend of her neck. She clung tighter.

There were no names gasped into the dark. No declarations. Just breath, heat, and the sound of two people surviving.

Their release came like a collapse. Unsteady. Unapologetic. The kind that leaves nothing standing. Her vision blurred, her chest heaved. His hand shook as he drew her closer. They stayed tangled—silent, breathless, and bare—under the weight of what had just been unspoken between them.

The air between them had changed. It wasn't love. It wasn't safety.

It was something else....Something irreversible.

✧ ✧ ◈ ◈ ◈ ◈ ✧ ✧

They laid entwined for long moments afterwards, the only sounds their ragged breathing slowly evening out and the faint whisper of the wind outside her window. The air was thick with the aftermath of their passion, heavy and intimate. Love felt boneless, drained, every nerve ending still tingling. Alexei shifted slightly, pulling the duvet higher over her bare shoulder, his arm tightening possessively around her waist.

She tilted her head back slightly, looking up at him in the dim light. His usual guardedness was gone, replaced by a raw vulnerability in his gaze, mixed with the lingering intensity of their coupling. "Alexei," she whispered, unsure what else to say, overwhelmed by the conflicting emotions churning inside her.

He simply brushed a damp strand of hair from her forehead, his thumb tracing the line of her cheekbone with surprising tenderness. "Sleep now," he said quietly, his voice husky. He pulled her closer, tucking her head against his chest, his own eyes closing as his breathing deepened, relaxing into sleep beside her.

"Lyubov moya," he whispered, just once.

Love laid curled against him, her cheek resting where his heart kept time like a clock she could never quite read. His scent clung to her skin—salt, breath, the echo of something once warm. The intimacy felt dangerous in its softness, seductive in its silence, too gentle to survive in the world they came from.

Behind her eyes, Ophelia's ghost stirred. The secrets, the warnings, the little fractures in truth she had willed herself not to see—they did not vanish. They watched from the corners, quiet and patient.

She had crossed into fire with open hands. Whatever part of her once demanded answers had gone quiet. The woman who lived for the truth was gone. In her place, a girl who wanted to believe in warmth more than she feared what it might burn.

Sleep came slowly, folding her into breath and heat and aching quiet.

As she closed her eyes, something inside whispered:

You won't wake up the same

Chapter 13:

Somewhere *In All The Mess, You Mattered.*

Love woke to light where he used to be.

The morning sun poured in through the gauzy curtains like it had something to prove. It illuminated the indentation in the mattress beside her—faint, fading, almost gone. She turned to it instinctively, half expecting warmth, a lingering presence, the brush of fingers against her spine. But there was only air. Cold. Unbothered.

Her skin still smelled like him. His cologne clung to the sheets, sharp and woodsy, softened by whatever alchemy had happened between them the night before. She reached for her phone. One message blinked back.

You're so peaceful when you're asleep. Thank you for last night, Love. More than I can say. Have unavoidable early commitments, but didn't want to leave without acknowledging... everything. Will call you at 12:30 PM.

—A

Acknowledging. It landed deeper than it should've. It was honest. Intentional. She read it again and again, like her brain needed proof it hadn't imagined the quiet gravity of last night.

Beside her phone, the orchid waited. A single bloom, white and precise. She didn't know where he'd gotten it, didn't ask why he'd left it. It was the kind of gesture that made no sense unless it was real. And God, she wanted it to be real.

She drifted through the morning in a daze. Tried to open Ophelia's case files, but the letters blurred. Her focus dissolved beneath flashes of memory—his mouth, his hands, the quiet vulnerability in his voice when the lights were off and the truth was harder to bury.

The morning passed quietly. Her desk stayed untouched. Ophelia's file remained closed. Every time she tried to focus, her thoughts betrayed her. They pulled back to the heat of his hand on her waist, the rasp in his voice when the lights were off, the breath he had stolen from her without even trying.

12:30pm came and went.

At first, she barely noticed. People got delayed. Especially people like him. Complicated people. Secretive people. Maybe he was trying to figure out how to speak honestly. That seemed harder for him than anything else.

By 2 o'clock, unease crept in.

Irritation was blooming quietly beneath her ribs. Alexei was meticulous. Intentional. He didn't strike her as the type to forget. Not unless he meant to. Not unless something was wrong....or he ghosted her AGAIN. Love, you're being a little crazy....he wouldn't do that...not after last night, she kept telling herself.

By 3pm, her fingers hovered over her screen longer than they should have. She typed out a message, reworded it twice, then hit send.

Hey, everything okay? Missed your call earlier.

Delivered. Not read.

That was when her chest started to close in. Not entirely. Just enough to make breathing feel mechanical.

She called once. Straight to voicemail. Again. Same thing.

The silence was no longer gentle. It rang in her ears like a warning bell.

She paced her bedroom, trying to remember exactly what he had said. The Brunswick redevelopment zone. The mill project. Some obscure site, half-forgotten. She hadn't cared at the time. He'd been touching her neck, and she hadn't listened. But now those details returned with perfect clarity.

At 4:17pm, her laptop lit up with a news alert.

Multi-Vehicle Collision Shuts Down Route 1 Near Brunswick Mill Redevelopment Zone

Dark grey SUV with out-of-state plates

Driver extricated with serious injuries

Transported to Maine Medical Center

She stopped reading.

She didn't have to finish it. She already knew.

The SUV was his. The location was exact. The silence suddenly made sense in the worst possible way.

She called James with fingers that shook so violently she almost dropped the phone.

"There's been an accident," she said as soon as he answered. "The place he mentioned, the SUV, the hospital. I think it's him. I know it's him."

James didn't question her. He didn't try to calm her with logic or doubt. He just asked where she was.

"Home."

"I'm coming now. Don't leave without me."

The drive was slow in the way time bends under panic. James kept one hand on the wheel, the other steady enough to be there if she needed it. He didn't fill the car with words. Just let her sit in silence and stare out the window, her arms wrapped tightly around herself like she could hold the fear inside and stop it from spilling everywhere.

She kept seeing flashes of Alexei's face. Not as he was last night, but as he might be now. Eyes closed. Bones broken. Blood she hadn't seen.

Hospitals smelled like endings.

◇ ◇ 🕮 ◇ ◇

The Maine Medical waiting room pressed down on her with its sterile lights and the kind of cold that seeped into the bones. Love didn't sit. She stood by the wall, arms crossed tightly over her chest, biting the inside of her cheek until she tasted the sharp tang of blood. Everything about this place felt wrong, too familiar, too much like the night Ophelia had disappeared behind a curtain of white sheets and never returned.

The triage nurse handed James a clipboard. He filled it out in quick, mechanical movements while Love stayed frozen in place, her body trembling in a rhythm she could not seem to break.

When the doctor appeared, Love barely registered the click of his shoes or the clipboard he carried. Only his voice cut through the fog.

"Family for Mr. Chervyakov?"

Her voice caught in her throat before she could force it free.

"I'm here," she said, thinner than she intended. "I mean, yes."

The doctor's expression remained unreadable. He only nodded.

"He's stable at the moment. Several broken ribs, significant internal bruising, a femur fracture that will need surgery, and a concussion. He is conscious in intervals but heavily medicated. He'll be admitted tonight."

Stable.

Not safe.

Not untouched.

Just breathing.

"Can I see him?"

The doctor nodded again. "Briefly. He may not be fully aware of what's happening. Just keep it calm."

James did not follow her. He only met her eyes, giving her a steady look, the kind that said without words that he would be there when she came back, no matter what version of herself she carried with her.

Love slipped past the curtain and into the low hum of machines.

Alexei lay motionless beneath the harsh hospital lights. His body was a collage of bruises and bandages, wires and tubes trailing from him like lifelines hastily sewn into a body that had come too close to disappearing. His leg was elevated. His face, normally so sharp and deliberate, was marred by swelling and cuts. His eyelids twitched, restless even in unconsciousness.

She moved closer, her steps soundless on the polished floor. She reached for his hand and touched it gently, afraid that even this small gesture might hurt him.

His skin was warm. Somehow, it mattered more than anything else.

She stood there for a long moment, breathing in sync with the machines. The steady beep. The low whisper of oxygen. Small, mechanical reminders that he was still here.

When she spoke, the words did not sound like her own.

"I thought you were gone."

The confession barely made it past her lips. It trembled there, fragile and raw.

She brushed her fingers along his knuckles, grounding herself in the pulse she could feel beneath his battered skin.

"I don't know what this is," she whispered. "I don't know what it's supposed to be. But the second I thought you were gone, my body remembered something before my mind could explain it."

Her breath hitched. She blinked hard against the burning in her eyes.

"I was scared."

The words felt heavier than anything else she had carried.

"You mattered," she said, quieter now, as if afraid that naming it out loud would somehow undo it. "Somewhere in all the mess, you mattered."

There was more she could have said. More she might have poured into the sterile air if she believed he could hold it. But this was not the moment for that. This was not the man who had smiled at her across crowded rooms, or kissed her like she was more than just grief and anger stitched into skin. This was only the shell, and she needed to believe the soul was still fighting to stay.

His fingers twitched beneath hers. Then, slowly, they closed around her hand, weak but unmistakable.

When the nurse came in and placed a hand on her shoulder, Love leaned down and pressed her lips to the back of his hand.

"I'm here," she said.

She slipped away before the tears won.

James was waiting when she emerged. He did not ask. She did not explain. They walked side by side through the sterile corridors and out into the night, carrying the unbearable knowledge that something fundamental had changed between heartbeats, and there was no going back now.

Chapter 14:

Oh **My God, I Love Him.**
The immediate aftermath of Love's whispered confession behind the curtain left her feeling hollowed out and strangely calm. The raw intensity of the emotion, forced out by terror and relief, settled within her not as a panic, but as a heavy, undeniable truth. She rejoined James in the corridor outside Treatment Bay 4, her face tear-streaked but her gaze steady. He didn't ask what happened, didn't press. He simply met her eyes with quiet understanding and offered a steadying hand on her arm as they walked back toward the main waiting area.

Oh my God, I love him.

The words echoed in her head, not as a revelation now, but as something settled. It was terrifying, yes, tangled inextricably with her grief for Ophelia and the mountain of unanswered questions surrounding Alexei himself, but it felt real. Solid. She hadn't said it to get a response. She had said it because it was the truth.

Soon, practicalities intruded. A hospital admissions clerk approached them kindly but efficiently.

"Mr. Chervyakov is being processed for admission," she explained. "We need some information, and more urgently, to notify next of kin. He didn't have any emergency contacts listed in his wallet, and his phone was damaged in the crash. Do you know who we should reach out to?"

Love felt that familiar, quiet ache of inadequacy.

"His mother is deceased," she said, voice low. "His father... lives abroad, I believe. Russia. I don't have contact information."

She remembered the mention of a half brother, but no name, no number. Nothing useful. The isolation hit her like a wave. For all his presence, his charm, his power, Alexei was here alone. Injured, confused, possibly facing surgery, and no one from his life knew except her.

James stepped in smoothly, his tone calm and helpful.

"His wallet and phone are probably with the police, since the vehicle was impounded. Once those are released, there might be contact information in them. In the meantime, his work—he mentioned international projects. Maybe checking corporate records for the Chervyakov name would lead to someone connected to his father. A main office line, maybe. It's not much, but it's a place to start."

The clerk nodded. "Thank you. We'll keep his status updated at the nurses' station if you think of anything else."

Love nodded. James's suggestion was logical. Impersonal, but useful. That was what James did well—finding a tether in the chaos.

Later, summoned by James, Ashton and Dahlia arrived, concern etched across their faces. Dahlia hugged Love immediately, arms tight and trembling.

"Oh, Love. James told us. That poor man. Are you alright? You look so tired, sweetheart."

Her worry for Alexei was genuine, but it was Love's face she was scanning for cracks.

Ashton stayed back a moment before quietly asking, "He's stable?"

Love nodded. "For now."

He said nothing more. Just gave a small nod and stood beside her.

Dahlia, after hovering near the nurse's desk for updates, went to fetch coffee. Ashton waited until she left before turning to Love.

"Honey," he said gently, "James filled us in. It sounds serious. This man... Alexei... He might be many things, but it seems like his life comes with some weight behind it. No local contacts, involved in a major accident... It raises questions. Not accusations, just... concern."

"I know," Love murmured. "Right now, I just need to know he's going to recover."

James returned then, slipping back into the circle with a slight frown.

"I just spoke with someone who monitored the EMS call logs when the crash came through. One of the responders noted very minimal skid marks at the scene. They think it might have been sudden brake failure, not a driver mistake."

Love blinked, the detail not fully sinking in. She nodded slowly. "Mechanical failure," she repeated.

It sounded like an explanation, like something simple.

But it didn't feel simple.

By that evening, Alexei had been moved upstairs. The surgical consult had been done. The leg would need work, soon. His vitals were stable, his head injury still under watch. Love sat at his bedside, the monitors soft and steady, the room dim and quiet.

She watched his chest rise and fall. Watched the way his hands lay, still bruised, one hooked with an IV, the other resting loosely at his side. His face was less pale than before, but the damage was still clear. The sharp lines of him muted by sleep and sedation.

Her parents, seeing she was calm again, eventually left. James lingered for a while, checked in with the nurse, then said gently, "Get some rest. You won't be any good to him if you're running on fumes. I'll talk to your internship, let them know what's happening."

Love nodded, but didn't move.

When James left, she shifted the chair closer and rested her hand on Alexei's forearm, just lightly.

The words she'd spoken still echoed in the silence.

I love you.

He hadn't heard them clearly. Maybe not at all.

But she had.

And that was enough.

The world outside—the case files, the shadows, the fear—felt far away in that moment. There was only this room, this steady breath, this broken man who had become her gravity.

She did not know what came next.

For now, she stayed.

Chapter 15:

Marginally Less Dramatic

The automatic doors of Maine Medical Center hissed apart, releasing Alexei into the late-winter chill like a breath held too long. The cold hit him immediately, a sharp reminder that the outside world hadn't paused with him. Love stood beside him, one hand light on his elbow as he adjusted to the crutches. After weeks inside the muted sterility of the hospital, everything felt jarringly real—the bite of wind, the watery glare of afternoon light, the low hum of traffic layered beneath birdsong.

He blinked slowly, pale against the sharp contrast of the sky. His posture was upright but guarded, as if bracing against more than just the cold.

James pulled the car to the curb and stepped out without ceremony, moving to open the trunk and retrieve the single duffel bag half-full, mostly with hospital-issue belongings and the few personal things Love had quietly brought him. "Ready?" he asked, not cold but carefully neutral.

Alexei nodded. "As I'll ever be." His voice was low, scratchy, the consonants slightly frayed around the edges. He offered James a brief glance of gratitude before settling into the passenger seat of Love's car, his movements stiff but deliberate. James would follow in Alexei's SUV, recently retrieved from the impound lot and barely holding itself together, much like its owner.

The drive downtown unfolded in a quiet that wasn't awkward, only thick with transition. Alexei stared out the window, watching familiar buildings scroll past like memories caught behind glass. Love drove carefully, occasionally glancing his way, noting the way his hand hovered near his injured leg. Protective. Tense.

"You okay?" she asked gently as they pulled into the parking garage beneath the sleek residential building.

His reply came after a pause. "Just adjusting. Re-entry feels... heavier than I expected."

❧ ✦ ❧ ❧ ✦ ❧ ❧ ✦ ❧ ❧ ✦ ❧

The apartment was as polished and controlled as everything else tied to Alexei. Wide, high ceilings. Concrete floors. Neutral colors. A wall of glass offered a sweeping view of the harbor, as though even the ocean had been curated to match the decor. The furniture was expensive and understated. The space looked lived-in only by furniture catalogues.

Love helped him to the sofa. The cushions were deep and firm, more functional than comforting. He lowered himself carefully, grimacing as he repositioned his leg onto the ottoman she nudged closer.

"Corporate lease," he muttered once the worst of the pain had passed. "Functional. Temporary. Cold."

His gaze traveled slowly across the room before settling on her again. "Thank you. For getting me home."

"Of course," she replied softly. She set her purse down on the pristine coffee table and crossed toward the kitchen. "Do you want anything? Water? Pain meds?"

"Water would help," he said, the tension still clinging to his shoulders. "Meds should be in the side pocket of the bag."

She moved through the apartment, opening drawers and cabinets that revealed very little. The fridge was nearly empty, stocked only with bottled water and a few forgotten condiments. Dishes were brand-new. Utensils untouched. A space without fingerprints.

Love returned with a bottle of water and the small orange vial. He took the pills with quiet gratitude, then leaned back with a sigh, closing his eyes like it took effort just to exist upright.

She hesitated for a moment. "I'll unpack your bag. Get things where you can reach them."

He nodded, eyes still closed.

She moved through the space silently. His bathroom was as sparse as the rest of the apartment, with clean lines and unopened products. She placed his toiletries carefully on the counter, arranged the clothes she had bought him into empty drawers, and charged his phone and laptop at the end table beside the couch.

The silence wasn't uncomfortable, only unfamiliar. There were no machines beeping. No nurses drifting in and out. No structure. Just the sound of his breath, the occasional city horn in the distance, and her own awareness of how intimately she'd come to understand this man without ever truly knowing him.

She stayed for the next hour, quietly organizing the kitchen, checking cupboards, finding filters for the coffee machine, noting what groceries he would need. Every so often, she glanced toward the couch, watching for the furrow in his brow, the flinch in his fingers when the pain crept back.

When he stirred again, blinking slowly, he looked less tense but undeniably worn.

"Sorry," he murmured.

"Don't be," she said, standing from where she'd been half-reading a book. "Are you hungry? I can go grab something. Soup?"

A faint smile passed across his face. "Soup sounds good."

That evening was the beginning of a new rhythm.

Love arrived after her classes and internship, always carrying something—groceries, warm food, a paperback novel. Alexei would usually be resting, sometimes working slowly through emails or pacing the length of the apartment on his crutches. He was quiet but present, the sharpness in his gaze returning gradually as the concussion's fog began to lift.

She cooked simple meals. Helped him with the awkward transitions of mobility. Kept track of his medication. It wasn't glamorous, but it was real. Intimate, in the kind of way that wrapped itself around mundane things.

They found a language in the silence.

✧ ✧

One afternoon, James checked in over the phone.

"How's he doing? Still brooding about the crutches?"

"Marginally less dramatic," Love said, her voice light. "He let me read Chekhov to him. Didn't complain once."

"Miraculous. And you? You're at his place more than your own lately."

"I'm fine. It's manageable."

There was a pause. Then James sighed, quiet and heavy.

"Clara had a rough night yesterday. Called me around three in the morning, just... spiraling. Panic attacks, crying, couldn't get her breathing under control."

Love sat up straighter, her concern immediate. "God, is she okay now?"

"Better. My mum's with her, and they've upped one of her medications. But I hate it. Being this far away. She doesn't talk to our parents the way she talks to me. She hides everything until it explodes." His voice faltered slightly. "It makes me feel like I'm failing her."

Love pressed her fingers to her temple, imagining the scene. Clara, fragile and overwhelmed, oceans away from the one person who seemed to understand her.

"She lives in the UK still? With your parents?"

"Yeah. They're in the countryside now. Peaceful, but isolating. And Clara's always been... delicate, emotionally. Brilliant, but easily overwhelmed. Therapy's on and off. Medication helps, then stops helping. I try to call regularly, but—" He paused again. "Sometimes I feel like I'm the only one holding the line for her."

"I'm sorry," Love said softly. "She's lucky to have you. Truly. If there's anything I can do..."

"Just keep yourself safe. That is the best thing you can do for me. I can't be worrying about the both of you."

"Trying my best," Love chuckled.

❈ ◇ ❈ ✧ ❈ ◇ ❈ ✧ ❈ ◇

Over the next few days, the apartment began to shift. Slowly. Subtly. A throw blanket over the couch. A cluster of Love's books beside the coffee table. Her scent in the kitchen. Her voice in the quiet.

One evening, while she worked through a complicated article for class, she asked his opinion. He listened carefully, brow furrowed, then launched into a breakdown so precise it took her breath away. The sharpness in him had not dulled, only hidden beneath exhaustion and injury. They talked easily for over an hour. It felt like remembering something they'd almost forgotten.

The physicality between them remained careful. Light touched when he needed help sitting up. Her hand on his back when the dizziness hit. Moments that passed quickly but lingered in her skin after.

She didn't know what this made them. Caregiver. Friend. Something softer. Something more.

But each night she spent in that apartment, folding his clean shirts into drawers, stirring soup over the stove, replacing the pillows when they fell, she felt it more clearly. He needed her. And she, somehow, needed this.

What had started as an emergency had become something else. Not a romance, not yet. But a kind of quiet partnership. A shared limbo. A recovery neither of them had chosen but both were navigating now. Together.

Chapter 16:

You Wrecked Me

Another week dissolved into the next. Outside Alexei's apartment, winter still pressed its cold hands against the city, but inside, a quiet warmth had begun to take root. He was moving better now—still dependent on crutches, but with steadier steps and fewer winces. He worked from his laptop in short bursts, often surrounded by documents she didn't recognize, half his conversations slipping into Russian or languages she couldn't place. Yet when she arrived, everything shifted. His eyes softened. His attention reoriented.

Evenings became familiar. Safe, even. Love would cook, adapting recipes from memory or half-read blogs, while Alexei sat nearby at the kitchen island, sipping water or just watching her like she was something calming he hadn't known he needed. The apartment smelled like garlic and rosemary instead of antiseptic. The silence held comfort, not tension.

One evening, a heavy snowfall muffled the city, the windows fogged with condensation, firelight flickering across the polished walls. They sat side by side on the sofa, wrapped in the hush of falling snow and memory.

Alexei's gaze lingered on the flames.

"My mother would've liked this," he said, almost to himself.

Love turned her head, listening.

"She hated pretense. Loud, irreverent. The kind of woman who drank red wine before noon and argued with art museum docents. She wore linen even in winter and refused to whisper anywhere." His voice softened. "She was the only warmth in our house growing up."

He paused, jaw tightening slightly.

"My father didn't know what to do with her. He loved her, I think, in his own clipped, transactional way. But she embarrassed him. Laughed too loud. Cried too openly. She wasn't afraid of being messy."

He glanced at Love, something unreadable in his eyes.

"She once threw a crystal decanter out the window during a dinner party. It shattered across the garden while my father was mid-sentence with a business partner. She didn't even blink. Just poured herself more wine from the bottle and said, 'Now that we've broken something, can we talk honestly?'"

Love huffed a surprised laugh.

"I loved her for that," he added quietly. "But I also learned early not to be like her. Not if I wanted to survive my father."

There was a beat of silence before he continued.

"When I was ten, he sent me to a boarding school in Switzerland. I didn't know until the day I left. She cried on the tarmac. I didn't. Not until the third night, when the lights were off and no one could hear."

Love's heart clenched.

"Did you get to come home for the holidays?"

"Not always. If the market was volatile, or there was some merger in Singapore or Dubai, I stayed behind. Some years, the staff would take turns bringing me soup and pretending they weren't being paid to care."

His voice was calm. Detached. But not unaffected.

"I learned how to say the right things. How to make people like me. But I never really trusted anyone. Not until..." He stopped, then shook his head lightly.

Love reached for his hand, lacing her fingers through his without hesitation.

"You don't have to keep earning love, you know."

He looked at her like that idea was a foreign language.

"You don't have to perform to be worth staying for."

His hand tightened around hers. Not forcefully. Just as if he needed to feel her there.

"And you?" he asked softly. "Who taught you silence?"

She exhaled slowly, like the answer had always been sitting on the edge of her throat.

"My sister. Ophelia."

She let the name linger in the room, felt the weight of it settle between them like it always did.

"She was the kind of person you orbit. You know? Loud, brilliant, reckless in ways that made everything feel bigger. She talked too fast. She took up space. I spent half my childhood trying to keep her grounded and the other half trying to catch up."

Alexei's gaze didn't leave her.

"She was freshly eighteen. Still had her whole life ahead of her. All of a sudden, she was losing weight, rebelling and arguing because we wouldn't let her stay out late. Typical teenager stuff, you'd think. I tried to ask if something was going on, but she didn't budge. A few days before she died, she looked happier somehow, although her face was paler than usual and her dark circles were more prominent. Then one night, she just didn't come home."

She didn't say more. Didn't need to. The silence that followed was enough.

"My dad shut down. My mom started pretending. And I—I learned how to disappear in plain sight."

Alexei didn't interrupt. Just listened, the way people do when they know what grief sounds like.

He shifted, then leaned forward like the words inside him had reached their limit.

"This thing between us," he said, voice frayed and low, "I don't know what it is anymore. I only know it's everything."

His breath shook, as though the weight of it was too much to carry any longer.

"I've spent my whole life mastering silence. I've built a goddamn fortress out of control. I have lived like a ghost in my own body, watching time pass through me. I've kissed people I can't remember. I've said the right words with a smile I borrowed from someone who never existed. But then you walked into my life like a rupture."

His hand found hers again, almost desperate.

"You shattered everything. I didn't fall in love with you. I collapsed into it. It wrecked me. You wrecked me."

He looked at her like she was the first sunrise after a century of dusk.

"When I was lying in that hospital bed, hovering between here and whatever comes next, I didn't see light. I didn't see God. I saw you. I heard your laugh. You weren't just the reason I stayed. You were the only thing left that felt like home."

His voice dropped to a whisper, reverent and ruinous.

"You are not a chapter in my story, Love. You are the language I didn't know I'd been dying to speak. You are the blood in my veins. You are every version of home I was never allowed to have."

Her chest ached. Her body shook with the effort of holding it all in.

"I don't just love you," he said. "That word isn't big enough. I am devoted to you. If the world burned, I would build you another with my bare hands. If I ever lose you, I will not survive it with dignity. I will fall apart completely."

He brought his forehead to hers, voice unraveling into air.

"You are the clearest thing I've ever seen. And I love you like it is killing me. And I would still choose it. Every time."

Her tears fell before her breath even caught.

She didn't speak. She didn't need to.

She kissed him like the world had stopped, because for them, it had...

And for the first time in a long time, neither of them was alone in the dark.

❖❖❖❖❖❖❖❖❖❖❖❖

Chapter 17:

He Isn't An Escape

Late winter reluctantly began to loosen its grip on Acadia Falls. Patches of stubborn snow lingered in the shadows, but the air held a hint of damp earth, and the afternoon sunlight filtering through the large windows of Alexei's apartment carried a touch more warmth. Inside, a new kind of thaw was occurring.

Weeks had passed since his return from the hospital, and a quiet, almost mundane rhythm had settled over Love and Alexei, replacing the tense atmosphere of crisis and recovery. The air no longer smelled like antiseptic or takeout. It smelled like coffee, garlic, and sleep shared between bodies that had grown used to each other.

Alexei, now walking without the cane and with only a slight favoring of his left leg, had regained most of his physical independence. Yet, the intimacy born during his recovery remained—transformed into something softer and quieter. They moved like people who had already survived something together.

Evenings were often spent in the kitchen. He had rediscovered his love of cooking and now insisted on making dinner most nights, though he would let her stir sauces or chop vegetables under watchful eyes. He teased her for how she held a knife, she teased him for lining up ingredients like he was about to perform surgery. Laughter came more easily in that apartment now. So did silence. And both felt safe.

She had started leaving small things behind. A scrunchie on the bathroom counter. A half-read book on the nightstand. Her favorite hoodie, draped over the back of his desk chair. Nothing intentional, but every item made the place feel a little more like theirs.

Sometimes in the mornings, she would wake to the smell of his cologne on the pillow beside her, the residual heat of where he had been. Other times, she would wake to him watching her quietly, like he was trying to memorize the way her face looked softened by sleep.

They didn't talk about love again. Not in words. It was there in how he tucked the blanket around her knees without her asking, how she made him tea the exact way he liked it without ever being told.

One night, they sat curled together on the couch, a half-empty wine glass in her hand, the soft hum of jazz floating through the speakers. Love rested her head on his chest, letting herself sink into the rhythm of his breathing.

"Tell me again," she murmured, eyes closed.

Alexei tilted his head slightly. "Tell you what?"

"How you found me."

He chuckled, low in his chest. "Still not over that, are you?"

"Nope," she said, smiling faintly. "I believe you. I just like hearing it."

He exhaled slowly, carding his fingers through her hair.

"As I said... I traced public data through a property research zone. Cross-referenced development permits. Tax rolls. I saw your family name, then yours. It wasn't a dramatic trail. Just one I was determined to follow."

She opened her eyes, staring ahead at the soft reflections of the city lights on the windowpane.

"But why?"

He was quiet for a moment.

"Because whenI left that night, something stayed with me. Something I couldn't name at the time. But it didn't let go. Not after a night. Not even after weeks."

He glanced down at her.

"You were not a moment to forget. And I've spent a lifetime forgetting people on purpose."

She looked up at him, lips parted slightly, and saw the truth written all over his face. That was the difference with him. He never oversold anything. But when he said something, it was meant.

She didn't reply. She didn't need to.

Instead, she reached for his hand and brought it to her chest, right over her heartbeat. And they stayed like that for a long time, in the low light, in the hush of something that felt like it might last.

A few days later, Love grabbed coffee with James near her internship. They sat at a quiet café tucked near a corner bookstore, the kind of place that served pour-overs in mugs too big for the saucers beneath them.

"He's really opening up," Love said. "Little pieces at a time. Not in speeches, but in small things."

James nodded, stirring honey into his tea.

"He'd be a fool not to," he said.

She raised an eyebrow.

"I mean it. You make people want to come out of hiding."

Love smiled softly, though her heart felt heavier than she expected.

"He's still complicated. But it's like he's trying."

James set his spoon down and leaned back slightly.

"My uncle worked briefly with one of Chervyakov Senior's holding firms. Said the man was... brilliant. But cold. Controlling. Built empires from the ground up but left emotional craters in his wake. That kind of childhood leaves marks."

Love looked down at her coffee.

"It does," she said.

James hesitated, then changed the subject.

"Clara's back in the clinic," he said quietly.

Love looked up sharply. "New one?"

"Yeah. In London. Expensive. Experimental. Mum's quietly falling apart. Dad's pretending we're all fine."

"I'm sorry, James."

He shrugged, but the weight of it didn't leave his face.

"Everyone's carrying something, yeah?" He glanced at her. "Just make sure he's carrying his own stuff. Don't let him hand it to you and walk away."

Love nodded, tucking the words away like a receipt.

◇ ❧ ◇ ❧ ◇

That night, when she got home, the house was still. Her parents were already seated at the table. The lights were dimmed, the table set with folded napkins and candles—trying, she thought, not to make it feel like an ambush.

She offered a soft hello and took her place. Dinner began with harmless chatter. Dahlia asked about her internship. Ashton asked if she was still considering writing something long-form about Ophelia one day. Love answered as best she could, but her thoughts drifted again and again to Alexei, to whether he had eaten, to whether his leg was aching.

After the dishes were cleared and Dahlia brought out plates of almond tart with sugared orange peel, Ashton leaned back in his chair.

"We've been meaning to talk," he said.

Love stilled her fork.

Dahlia glanced at her husband, then at Love, lips pressed together like she already regretted letting him speak first.

"It's about Alexei," Ashton continued. "You're spending most nights at his apartment. You're rarely home. And we still know next to nothing about him."

Love looked down at her tart. Suddenly, it felt far too sweet.

"He was in an accident," she said. "I was helping."

"Is that still what it is?" he asked. "Helping?"

She didn't reply.

"We're not judging, sweetheart," Dahlia said gently. "It just feels... fast."

"I know him," Love said. "Better than anyone else has in a long time."

Ashton studied her.

"Does he know you?"

Love met his eyes.

"He tries. Every day."

There was a long silence.

"You've been through a lot," Ashton said. "We just want you to be sure that what you're building with him is something real. Not something built on survival instinct."

Love opened her mouth, then closed it again.

"You think I'm chasing comfort," she said finally.

Ashton met her gaze. "I think you're grieving, and grief is clever. It knows how to disguise itself as purpose."

That struck something in her, but she wouldn't let it show.

"Alexei isn't an escape," she said. "He's the first thing that's made me want to stay."

Her father's jaw shifted. Not approval. Not agreement. Just the quiet weight of not knowing how to protect someone who had already stepped past the boundary.

Love pushed her chair back, not angry, just tired.

"I have to go," she said. "I told him I wouldn't be late."

Dahlia stood and hugged her quickly, whispering something about taking care of herself.

Ashton watched her leave, his expression unreadable.

The following weeks unfolded like a soft blur. Alexei's apartment slowly shed its corporate shell and began to feel lived in. A throw blanket Love bought ended up draped over the couch. Her books started collecting near the window seat. Her scent clung to the pillows. His schedule adjusted around her presence like it had always been part of the architecture.

On Friday, she returned from work to find the air filled with the warm smell of seared garlic and citrus. Alexei stood at the stove, focused, plating scallops with a sprig of thyme. The same dish from their first dinner at The Mariner's Table.

She smiled without even taking her coat off.

"You're ridiculous," she said.

"I try," he replied, setting down the plates.

They ate by candlelight, not out of romance, but because they had forgotten to change the kitchen lightbulb.

That weekend, they drove north up the coast, the windows cracked, the salty wind filling the car. They stopped at a cove she had loved as a child, sat on a weathered bench, and ate lobster rolls wrapped in paper.

After they finished eating, Love stood and wandered toward the rocky edge of the shore, her boots crunching over frostbitten pebbles. The wind tugged her hair into her face, and for a moment, she let it. She stared out at the water, the cold biting her cheeks, trying to understand what it meant to feel still inside her body after so long. Behind her, she heard Alexei's slower footsteps.

He didn't speak right away. Just stood beside her, close enough that their arms brushed.

"I used to hate the ocean," he said, surprising her.

She glanced over. "You? With your yacht-owning father?"

He smirked. "Exactly. Every moment near the water felt like a performance. Yacht clubs. White linen. Forced smiles. I never actually listened to the waves. Never realized they had their own kind of language."

Love looked back toward the sea. "What are they saying now?"

"That not everything needs to be claimed. Some things just want to be witnessed."

She let that settle.

Love told him about the time Ophelia almost fell off the rocks trying to take a picture, how their mother had screamed so loud the birds scattered. He had laughed, quietly, then reached for her hand and held it as if she had just handed him something precious.

They did not rush. They did not define anything, but the shape of their days grew more certain.

Still, in the quiet moments, Love sometimes wondered if this happiness could last. If she deserved it. If Alexei's shadows had truly settled, or just gone still for a while...

But she didn't ask those questions out loud.

She let herself breathe.

She let herself believe.

Beneath the surface, the fault lines waited.

Still and quiet.

Chapter 18:

Catch Moonlight In A Jar

The late afternoon sun slanted through the large windows of Alexei's apartment, casting long shadows across the polished concrete floor. Love sighed, dropping her bag onto a chair and kicking off her heels. She walked straight over to where Alexei sat reading on the sofa and collapsed beside him, her body folding into his like it had been waiting all day to return.

"Rough day?" he asked, immediately lowering his book. His arm curled around her without hesitation.

"Beyond rough," she groaned, nuzzling into the familiar warmth of his sweater. "You know that investigative piece I've been digging into on the city council rezoning permits? The one involving Councilman Davies?"

Alexei nodded. "The one with the suspected backroom deals?"

"Exactly. Well, I finally got Davies' former aide to agree to an off-the-record background chat today. Took weeks to build that trust. We meet, she's nervous but talking—actual specifics. Names. Dates. It was gold, Alexei."

She sat up, the frustration in her voice giving her posture an edge. "Then her phone rings. It's Davies. Pure 'coincidence,' apparently. And suddenly she clams up. Starts backpedaling. Says she misspoke, that she was speculating. It vanished. Right in front of me."

She leaned forward, her fingers raking through her hair. "He must have warned her. Or scared her. I don't know. Trying to pin down the truth with people like that, people protecting their own skin..."

She paused, her voice tight with fury. "It's like trying to nail Jell-O to a wall. Infuriating. And hopeless."

Alexei listened intently, his expression quiet and thoughtful. He reached out, tucking a strand of hair behind her ear, his touch steady.

"I understand the frustration," he said, voice low. "Dealing with people who prioritize self-preservation above all else... it demands a kind of tenacity that devours you over time." He leaned back, eyes on something distant. "Sometimes, wrestling with invisible barriers, trying to grasp what's deliberately hidden... it feels like trying to catch moonlight in a jar."

The phrase dropped so effortlessly that it took a beat to register. And then it hit.

Love froze.

Her breath stuttered. Her body went still. Her pulse thudded in her ears.

Catch moonlight in a jar.

She hadn't heard that in over a year. Whimsical. Melancholy. Utterly Ophelia.

It was a phrase only her sister used. A strange little metaphor Love had always found haunting and beautiful. Something soft and private, something that lived in a notebook or a whispered late-night conversation. And now it was here, surfacing like a ghost in Alexei's mouth.

She stared ahead, her face neutral. But inside, something began to unravel.

"...an impossible task, designed to make you question your own efforts," Alexei continued, entirely unaware of the explosion he had just set off inside her chest.

It was like a match dropped into kerosene. The words scorched through her, uninvited and familiar in a way that made her stomach turn. Her sister had said that. Her sister only. And now it was here, in the low light, surrounded by the scent of sage and candle wax and comfort, cracking her world open.

She forced herself to smile. A small, tight thing.

"Yeah," she murmured, voice paper-thin. "Something like that."

She needed to breathe. Needed to get out from under it. The weight. The memory. The implication.

"So," she said quickly, too brightly, "forget my disastrous day. How was yours? Any breakthroughs on the structural analysis front?"

He nodded, and she barely registered it, her thoughts sinking into a hollow so deep it swallowed even her own voice.

◇ ⚓ ◇ ⚓ ◇

That night, after dinner and a slow descent into bed, she lay beside him in the dark. His arm draped across her waist, the rise and fall of his breath warm against the nape of her neck. But she couldn't sleep. She couldn't close her eyes.

Catch moonlight in a jar.

The phrase echoed, echoing in a loop that scraped along her ribs. She could hear it in Ophelia's voice, soft and whimsical. She could hear it in Alexei's voice, deep and accidental. She could hear them overlapping. Merging.

By morning, the silence inside her had curdled into something cold and coiled.

When Alexei immersed himself in a string of calls—his tone sharp, rapid, some of it in clipped Russian—Love mumbled something about needing to pick up research materials for her internship.

He didn't question it. He just kissed her temple and went back to work.

She drove home under a slate-gray sky, gripping the steering wheel so tightly her knuckles ached. The moment she stepped into her parents' house, a strange stillness settled over her. The kind of silence that felt curated, like the air had been holding its breath for too long.

She made her way to Ophelia's room. Nothing had changed. The room was exactly as she left it—too clean, too preserved. A museum for a girl who no longer existed.

Love stood in the doorway for a long time, staring at the neatly made bed, the untouched bookshelf, the collection of sun-faded art postcards pinned above the desk. She felt like a trespasser in her own grief.

She moved slowly, almost reverently, and began her search. First the obvious things—diaries she had already skimmed a dozen times. She flipped through pages filled with Ophelia's sarcastic wit, her glittering mind, her signature loops of ink. Nothing. No mention of the phrase. No confirmation. Just the familiar ache of reading her sister's voice trapped in past tense.

She dug deeper. Sketchbooks, school folders, old birthday cards tucked in a shoebox. Still nothing.

After an hour, her limbs ached. She sat back on the floor, surrounded by open notebooks and flipped pages, and pressed her palms to her eyes.

What am I doing?

She felt unhinged. Like she had slipped down into a pocket of obsession and couldn't find her way out. Maybe it wasn't her phrase. Maybe she never even said it. *Maybe I've built an entire theory around a poetic coincidence.*

The weight of her own suspicion began to turn inward. She felt pathetic. Twisted.

Why am I trying to ruin something good? Why am I clawing at a thread just because I'm scared of being happy?

Alexei had been nothing but patient. Present. Devoted. He had held her during panic attacks, remembered how she liked her tea, traced poems on her bare shoulder with his fingertip when he thought she was asleep.

What if I'm the one breaking this?

She wanted to stop. To pack everything away and drive back to him. To say nothing. To pretend it was a fleeting shadow and not something real, but her hands moved anyway.

A box under the bed caught her attention. She'd seen it before. She thought she had gone through it. But when she opened it, a few books sat awkwardly against the side, the weight uneven, like something had slipped between them.

She reached in, moving aside a crumpled flyer and a dog-eared copy of Wuthering Heights, and felt paper slide against her fingers.

A single, folded sheet. Lined paper. Handwritten. Familiar ink.

Her breath caught as she unfolded it slowly.

It wasn't neat. It wasn't a journal entry. It was a brainstorm. A scatter of phrases, arrows, scribbled thoughts. Symbols. Circles. Words underlined and scratched out and rewritten, buried in the middle of a swirling mess of half-thoughts and tangled lines.

"*...like trying to catch moonlight in a jar. Impossible beauty. He understands this, I think. The impossibility. Maybe that's why...*"

Her heart dropped into her stomach.

She read it again, and again. As if the paper might change its mind and erase what it had written.

He understands.

Not I. Not we.

He.

She stared at the word until it blurred.

Everything went still.

This was not a coincidence. Not a dream. Not her grief projecting.
Alexei had known Ophelia...and he had lied.

Chapter 19:

He Understands This

Love hadn't been in this room in weeks. Not since Alexei. Not since things started unraveling with too much force to hold. The sunlight through the blinds split the air into pale stripes, falling across a carpet that hadn't been stepped on since before the funeral. Scarves hung loosely from the back of the desk chair. Candles, melted and blackened, sat like relics on the windowsill. Notebooks leaned against textbooks in precarious towers. The room looked untouched, preserved, but wrong. It was a bedroom pretending to be whole.

Love stepped in with the weight of breath she hadn't taken. She didn't know why she was here again. She had already found the journal. Already cried into the pages. She wasn't looking for new evidence. Not anymore. She was returning to the scene of a feeling.

She walked slowly, eyes gliding over shelves, the mirror, the bed still slightly indented from where Ophelia used to nap. This wasn't about discovery. It was about remembering the person who once lived inside this space. She sat down near the window, hands in her lap, and allowed herself to breathe in the sadness that clung to the walls. It wasn't loud grief. It was quiet. The kind that sets up residence in your spine.

He understands this.

An echo of what she had read violated her thoughts.

✧ ✧ ✧

THE NEXT HOURS BLURRED. She moved without purpose, without direction. She found no new clues, no revelations. Only echoes. Only reminders of what she couldn't unsee anymore.

Later that evening, she met James at their usual bar. He was already seated, coffee in hand, expression unreadable but waiting. She didn't sit. She paced, hands knotted in the sleeves of her sweater.

"I need more," she said finally, stopping in front of him.

"You already have the journal," James said.

Her voice lowered. "That's not enough."

His gaze searched hers for a moment. "What do you think is missing?"

"The truth," she said, barely above a whisper. "The autopsy was redacted. Sterile. Sanitized. The real story has been erased."

James rubbed the edge of his cup. "You think there's something worse in the version they didn't release."

"I don't think. I know."

He nodded once, but his eyes shifted. There was something behind them. A tension.

She tilted her head. "Can you get it?"

James hesitated. "It won't come through official channels. I have someone in records. She owes me. A favor for a favor."

Love said nothing. Just watched him.

"I'll keep your name out of it," he added. "But this will be the kind of file that isn't traceable. Don't expect a formal header."

When he returned later that night, he handed her a plain envelope. No markings. No seal. Just weight.

She opened it, the pages cold in her hands.

Fetal tissue detected. Estimated six to eight weeks gestation. Internal recommendation: information to be withheld from family report.

Her breath hitched. Her hands tightened around the edges of the paper.

"She was pregnant," she said. Not in shock. In fury.

James exhaled slowly. "They didn't tell your parents. Marked it as nonessential."

She looked up at him, eyes glassy but unflinching. "That's not nonessential. That's everything."

He didn't argue. There was nothing to argue.

She stepped back from the table. Her voice had a tremor. "This wasn't negligence. It was protection. Someone didn't want her story to exist."

"Love," James started, but she didn't wait.

"I have to confront him."

James stood too quickly, hands on the table. "You can't."

"I need to ask. I need to see what he says. What he does when I ask."

"You don't know what he's capable of," James said.

She turned to him. "I don't think he'd hurt me."

"You didn't think he'd lie either."

Silence stretched between them.

◈ ◈ ✦ ◈ ◈

She went home, but she didn't rest. The night was too still, and her mind too loud. She sat in front of her laptop, face lit by the screen, hands moving automatically. She wasn't searching for proof. She was gathering it. Documenting the unspeakable. Naming the unnamed.

Old folders. Encrypted backups. Temp files from devices she and Alexei had once shared without thinking. Data fragments surfaced like bones in thawing snow. She opened them slowly, methodically. She didn't cry. She didn't pause.

One file appeared. Damaged. Fragmented. Time-stamped two days before Ophelia died.

O. confirmed. Discretion locked. Meet at 11. Archive cleared. Alpha protocol if compromised.

Her pulse didn't spike. It sank. Alpha protocol. She had heard him say that phrase once, laughing. She'd thought it was a joke.

Another line emerged. This one dated the morning after Ophelia's death.

Unavoidable. Resolution complete. Damage managed. Silence holds.

She didn't need a name. The rhythm of that language, the structure—it belonged to him. She recognized it the way you recognize someone's voice in the dark.

She created a folder and named it "Eclipse". It wasn't poetic. It was precise. An eclipse doesn't simply darken. It conceals the very thing meant to illuminate. Into it, she placed everything—screenshots, documents, the pregnancy confirmation, her questions, her fear.

Not for justice.

For readiness.

Her phone buzzed. The screen lit up.

Alexei: *You've been quiet. Everything okay? Miss you.*

Her fingers hovered, then typed.

Just tired. I'll call you later.

She pressed send. Closed the laptop like it was a casket, and sat.

Not angry. Not broken.

Just waiting.

Like the storm hadn't yet arrived, but the sky already knew.

Chapter 20:

Starting Small

Love woke before him now, not because of fear or instinct, but because the silence in her body was louder than the warmth of sleep. She lay still in the half-light of dawn, listening to the hum of the apartment, to the subtle creak of pipes, to the shallow rhythm of Alexei's breath beside her. The weight of his arm across her stomach might have once comforted her. Now, it pinned her.

She counted backward from thirty, just to center herself, and then slipped free from beneath the covers, padding across the cold floor to the kitchen. Her hands moved automatically, scooping coffee grounds, heating the kettle, adding the precise splash of cream to his mug. These little rituals gave her just enough space to breathe.

On the surface, everything remained unchanged. She made breakfast. He kissed the corner of her mouth. They exchanged idle conversation about the news, about some minor logistics delay in Switzerland, about how Maine felt colder than usual this spring. His phone buzzed constantly now. She never asked who was on the other end. She didn't need to.

While he muttered clipped phrases into the phone in Russian and French, and sometimes English with a sharper accent than usual, Love sat across from him at the dining table and pretended to read an article on her laptop.

In reality, she was scrolling through LLC registries, local government archives, and planning board hearing minutes. Her tabs were disguised under layers of misdirection. A real estate report. A grant proposal for a community garden. A cached blog post about New England's top-ranked independent journalists. She had learned how to hide her intent beneath three layers of polite curiosity.

The Geneva hit had landed exactly how she wanted. Not all at once. Not explosively. But slowly, like rot beneath marble. His father was furious. His tone on calls had shifted from irritation to something more clipped. He had taken a late-night walk two days ago, something he never did, and returned with his jaw clenched, hair wet from rain, face unreadable. Love had been sitting on the couch, curled in the throw blanket, eyes on her screen. He hadn't said a word. Just poured himself a drink and stood staring out at the harbor lights until his shoulders finally dropped.

She told him she was sorry about the stress. That she hated seeing him this tense. That he deserved peace. She rubbed the back of his neck while he sat hunched at his laptop and whispered that he didn't have to carry it all alone.

He thanked her. He said he didn't know what he would do without her.

She smiled and brought him tea.

Then, when he left for a quick meeting downtown the next day, she walked over to his laptop and took her time.

She didn't need passwords anymore. Not when she had already memorized his browser history, his preferred folder structure, the names he used for internal documents, the files he deleted but forgot to scrub from the cache. She didn't steal anything outright. That would be reckless. But she took notes. Quiet ones. Enough to understand which subcontractor had falsified a soil report. Enough to identify the code name of a site that was quietly being rebranded under a new LLC. Enough to know that someone had been paid under the table to expedite a variance that should have taken months.

She closed everything when she was done, wiping the dust from the keys with her sleeve.

◇ ✦ ◇ ✦ ◇

Later that night, she let him rest his head in her lap while they watched a documentary about ocean acidification. She ran her fingers through his hair and asked if he'd ever been sailing off the coast of Norway. He said yes, once, years ago, and told her a story about nearly capsizing in a storm. She laughed in all the right places and pretended not to notice the hollowness in his voice when he described the cold.

She didn't go after him directly next. That would be too obvious. She knew better now. Real sabotage didn't look like confrontation. It looked like clumsy mistakes. Bad luck. Accidents of timing.

She started small.

She removed one number from his contact list and replaced it with another. Just one digit. A single shift that redirected a planned call to the wrong extension. When he snapped at a junior associate over miscommunication, Love offered soft, disapproving silence, the kind that made him question himself just enough to apologize.

She moved his documents. Never far. Just a few inches to the left on the desk. Reversed their order in the printer tray. Misaligned the margins of a legal letter and left it folded wrong in his briefcase. He didn't blame her. Of course not. But she saw the moment his hand hovered over his schedule the next morning, the tiny pause before he scanned for what felt off.

She stopped answering questions directly. When he asked if she'd seen his red folder, she said she thought she had, maybe, by the door — wasn't it near the keys? If he asked what she wanted for dinner, she'd tell him she wasn't sure anymore. If he kissed her cheek, she'd smile, but sometimes she wouldn't meet his eyes. Just once in a while. Just enough to plant the idea.

She began to water the orchid he'd bought her twice a day, knowing it only needed it once. It withered in the kitchen window within a week.

He noticed, but didn't say anything.

She replaced it with a cactus.

At Channel 5, she stayed late again, this time actually reviewing footage. Not for a story, but to harvest sound bites — little pieces of dialogue from old council meetings, from planning hearings where men in suits spoke too fast and too vaguely. She clipped them into folders labeled "**INTERNAL**: *Segment Leads*" and stored them on a drive that she kept in her coat pocket, never on the cloud.

She visited the town library, not for books, but for their microfilm records. Scanned pages of mill redevelopment notices, maps, proposals that dated back before Alexei had even arrived. She noted where the names had changed, where companies had vanished from one filing to the next. She created a timeline. It was ugly, and full of gaps, but it was just ugly enough to raise questions if given to the right person.

And she already knew who that person was.

He started locking his briefcase again.

She noticed when he left his keys in his jacket instead of his usual hook by the door. She noticed the slight hesitation before he left his tablet on the charger overnight. He was beginning to wonder. She could see it in the way he watched her when she entered the room — how he waited half a second longer to answer simple questions, as if testing her tone, measuring her words against something unspoken.

Their intimacy thinned.

He still kissed her, still touched her back as she passed him in the hallway, but the pressure in his fingers had changed. He wasn't reaching for comfort anymore. He was reaching for confirmation. For something that still felt real.

She gave it to him. Slowly, deliberately.

She cooked his favorite meal one night. Set the table with candles. Wore the soft sweater he had once said made her look like a home he didn't deserve.

Across the table, in the amber light, he looked at her the way people look at promises they are desperate to believe in.

He kissed her hand and told her she made him feel seen. That no one else had ever fit him like she did — like a key turned quietly in the right lock.

She smiled and kissed his knuckles, telling him she loved hearing him say things like that.

He never noticed the tremor in her hands.

He didn't notice the way her smile held, just a second too long.

That night, while he showered, she tucked a folded slip of paper into the lining of her coat. No label. No signature. Just a cryptic set of initials and dates, tucked where he might find it if he came home early enough.

If he noticed, he said nothing.

Two nights later, he woke up gasping from a nightmare he couldn't name.

She gathered him against her chest, whispered it was just a dream, smoothed her hand down his spine until he sank back into uneasy sleep.

He still loved her. Trusted her. Let her pick up his jacket when he dropped it. Let her answer his buzzing phone once when his hands were full of groceries.

He smiled through all of it, even when a flicker of hesitation crossed his face. Even when the ground began to shift beneath his feet and he didn't know why.

She hadn't shouted. She hadn't confessed. She hadn't done anything that couldn't be explained away.

She had simply become the silence between his thoughts.

The splinter under his skin.

The shadow at the edge of the bed that never quite touched him — but never quite left either.

He still kissed her goodnight.

He still whispered her name.

He just didn' always believe it when she whispered his back.

Chapter 21:

Love, She's Cold.

The fallout from the environmental blog post did not crash down all at once. It seeped in quietly, disguised at first as harmless background noise, almost indistinguishable from the static of bureaucratic delays. Over a few days, that static sharpened into interference. Emails from board members grew clipped, callbacks stretched longer, and a town manager who had once spoken in vague pleasantries sent a memo back with the phrase "potential re-evaluation" circled twice in heavy red pen.

Alexei did not speak about it. He wore the pressure the way he wore everything, neatly and silently, like an extra layer stitched into his clothes. Only Love noticed the shifts: the harder snap of his laptop closing after midnight, the stiffness in his shoulders at dinner, the second too long his gaze lingered whenever she typed at her computer. He never asked what she was working on, and she never gave him reason to. She fed him easy lies about her coursework, her internship projects, her midterms. Her life became a careful choreography, cluttered with just enough real deadlines to drown out suspicion.

She still kissed him goodbye in the mornings and brought him coffee in the evenings. She still curled beside him on the couch and laughed at old black-and-white movies. Yet all of her real work happened in the quiet spaces between.

Love spent afternoons at the town clerk's office, slipping extra copies of permit records into her folders with apologetic smiles. She cross-referenced contractor filings in university libraries, logging hours of research on public computers where no trace could link back to her. Every piece tightened the noose she was weaving around him.

Another anonymous tip landed in a journalist's inbox, this time attaching soil inconsistencies connected to the Brunswick project. The story unfurled like smoke across activist forums and local pages. His name was not printed in bold. It did not have to be.

She read the article while stirring cold tea with a pen, her notebook open in front of her as she pretended to study. When Alexei walked into the kitchen, grim and wary, asking if she had seen the news, she lifted her head slowly, shook it once, and murmured that she had not had time.

He believed her.

That night, Alexei did not rage. He did not accuse. He simply grew quieter, the way a man does when he begins to realize the ground beneath his feet has started to rot.

Love dismantled him piece by piece, in ways too subtle to trace. One morning she unplugged his tablet charger just enough to leave it dead during a critical meeting, and when he returned home, frustrated and fuming, she suggested sweetly that the outlet might need replacing. Another afternoon she reordered the folders in his briefcase so that signed contracts were hidden behind drafts, forcing him to stumble awkwardly in front of a client. When he grumbled about the inconvenience, she kissed the corner of his mouth and told him he was working too hard.

At his request, she started responding to some of his emails—simple RSVPs, appointment confirmations—until the day she intentionally misdirected a message to one of his competitor's assistants. It was not enough to accuse, not enough to prove, but just enough to leave behind a whiff of suspicion.

She pieced together a video montage from council meetings, splicing together moments where officials contradicted themselves about the Mill Zone development. The footage carried no accusations, only questions. The kind that stains a name more permanently than any proof.

The video spread like wildfire, but Alexei never mentioned it. He barely touched his food that night, or even spoke. He still fell for her lies. He was bleeding out and he didn't even know it.

James called her the following Tuesday, and the moment she heard his voice, Love knew something had broken. His words came in gasps, cracked and raw. Clara had missed her therapy session again. Love promised she would check in, even swore she would cut her study session short, but she never left the scaffolding of her revenge.

She told herself there would be time tomorrow.

There was not.

That night she planted another decoy, a slip of fake notes mentioning investigative sourcing and ethical risks, left just visible enough in her work bag for Alexei to find. He discovered it the next morning but said nothing, only pressed it into her hand with a look she could not decipher.

Alexei stayed home the next day. He rescheduled calls to linger closer to her. His touch was still warm, his arms still wrapped around her at night, but tension threaded through the space between their bodies. A subtle, constant tightening. He kissed her hair and murmured promises in the dark, yet every time she shifted, every time she stayed in the bathroom too long, she could feel him listening.

Love smiled through it. She kissed him and told him he was her peace. She whispered that she loved him as if it were still true.

Later that night, she quietly deleted one of his old saved contacts and replaced it with a name from a chapter he thought he had closed long ago. Just to see if he would notice.

🐌 ◈ ◇ 🐌 ✦ 🐌 ◈

The storm came late Thursday afternoon while she was sitting at his kitchen table pretending to edit internship footage. Her phone vibrated across the table, and James's voice tore through the line, broken and desperate.

"Love... oh God... I just got home... Uncle David's away... Clara... she didn't make it to art therapy... I found her... there's pills... a note..."

His sobs filled the silence that fell over her like ash.

She snapped to her feet, the laptop forgotten, words spilling from her mouth too fast to sound real. "James, stay on the line. Where are the paramedics?"

"Coming," he rasped, voice cracking. "She wrote... she couldn't stand the noise anymore..."

He choked out one last word before falling silent. *Karma.*

The word hooked itself into her chest with vicious claws.

There was no time to think. No time to pick apart the cruelty of it. She slammed her laptop shut, grabbed her keys, and sprinted out the door.

As she drove toward James's house, heart hammering against her ribs, another thought, cold and undeniable, whispered its way into her mind. James would be broken. Utterly shattered by grief. He would not have the strength to see her clearly anymore. He would not be able to question her.

The thought should have sickened her.

Instead, it settled somewhere deep inside, alongside every other monstrous thing she had buried there.

The serpent inside her had stopped whispering.

It had learned how to smile.

Chapter 22:

C lara Was Gone

The street looked unreal under the wash of emergency lights, like a crime scene reconstructed for television. Red and blue flickered against damp hedges, bouncing off windows, casting shadows that didn't belong. Love moved through it like a ghost, barely feeling the wind biting at her coat. She saw James long before she reached him. He was crouched on the lawn, his arms hanging loose at his sides, his eyes wide and vacant as if staring straight through everything and everyone. The paramedics near the door had already slowed. Their movements were too calm. Too rehearsed.

Clara. was. gone.

A police officer's voice murmured confirmation — low, professional, apologetic. It barely registered. The sound of it was obliterated by the way James collapsed, his knees hitting the grass with a dull thud, his body folding like a paper crane crushed in a closed fist. There were no screams, no words, just this raw, gasping silence that twisted inside Love like a jagged hook.

The hours after blurred into something grey and airless. She was aware of Layla at some point, of David Harrison standing still and grim like a man who had seen grief before and stopped trying to run from it. The house was cold. The police tape flapped in the wind. Inside, the world had stopped turning.

James's parents arrived the next day, pale and trembling. His mother looked like her bones had forgotten how to hold her upright. His father said very little, clasped James by the shoulder, and wept in silence. James himself remained adrift. He didn't cry so much as unspool. He would pace for hours then sit for ten seconds before standing again. He refused to sleep.

Refused food. At times, he'd grip Love's arm with a desperation that startled her, his voice dropping into strange, broken fragments.

"She said the silence was too loud... like it was listening to her... I thought she was just tired."

"She kept saying it was poisoned. Everything. Every word anyone said."

"You have to be careful, Love. You have to promise. Don't trust too easily. Not anymore."

Love nodded, stroked his hair, whispered reassurances she didn't believe. The guilt settled in her gut like something rotting. She hadn't seen Clara in weeks. Hadn't checked in. Hadn't noticed the shadows growing darker around her. She'd been too deep in her quiet, ruthless war, too obsessed with Alexei's downfall to see anything else. That failure nested inside her now like a second heart.

When she called Alexei, his voice was gentle, low, and almost unbearably kind.

"My Love, I'm so sorry. I know how much James means to you... and Clara. I can't imagine. If you need to step away from the internship, from everything, I'll take care of it. You shouldn't have to manage this alone. Let me help."

He didn't press her. Didn't ask questions. Just stayed steady. Empathetic. Everything she'd once fallen for. She thanked him softly, hung up, and stood alone in her room for a long time, staring at her reflection like it was someone else's face.

▭ ▭ ▭ ▭ ▭

The funeral was held two days later, beneath a sky the color of bruised porcelain. The chapel was quiet, full of tightly drawn faces and flowers that smelled too strong. James stood beside his parents, unmoving. A portrait of Clara sat near the altar — a recent one, taken in better days, her smile still real, still untouched.

After the service, a muted reception unfolded in Uncle David's house. Love stayed near James, gently guiding him to sit, to drink water, to answer people without having to think. Even Layla looked subdued, her usual glitter replaced with smudged mascara, curls half-tamed in a messy braid, trying to manage condolences and greetings.

After a while, she appeared again beside Love, a hand lightly brushing her sleeve.

"Hey," Layla said in a hushed tone. "There's someone here I wanted you to meet. He's... kind of connected to all of us, in a roundabout way."

He stood tall, polished in a way that spoke of old money but without the arrogance that usually followed. His navy coat was immaculately tailored, every line precise, as if he had been sewn into it. The black shoes he wore gleamed under the dim light, untouched by anything so ordinary as dirt. His eyes, a muted gray, held a sharpness dulled only by habit — the look of someone who noticed far too much and had taught himself how to pretend otherwise. His presence did not shout. It did not even whisper. It simply filled the space around him with a stillness so heavy, it became impossible not to look.

"Love," Layla said, nudging her gently, "this is Felix Sinclair. His family manages the Sinclair property — you know, the one where that huge winter party? Felix, this is my best friend, Love Godfrey."

Felix extended his hand, his smile warm but measured. "It's good to finally meet you," he said. "James speaks highly of you. I'm sorry we're meeting under these circumstances. He also mentioned you lost your sister as well. I'm truly sorry for your loss."

Love shook his hand, offering a small, polite smile, though her fingers stiffened at the mention of Ophelia. His tone was easy, natural, the kind of conversation meant to bridge strangers without lingering too long, but the crack had already been made.

As Felix turned and gave a brief nod toward James, moving to murmur something quietly to David before slipping into the night, Love stayed frozen a second longer than necessary. Her chest felt tight, as if some invisible hand had pressed down hard enough to bruise.

Layla let out a slow breath beside her.

"I don't know," she whispered. "He seems...fine, right? I mean, James trusts him. Still, there's something about him that feels... off. Like he's too... composed."

Love didn't answer.

Her eyes stayed fixed on the door Felix had walked through, a quiet tightness settling in her chest.

He had said all the right things.
Exactly the right things.
Maybe that was what unsettled her.
Or maybe it was nothing. Maybe grief was making ghosts of strangers.
❖ ❖ ❖ ❖ ❖ ❖ ❖

Chapter 23:

S ilence Hides Things

The days after Clara's funeral dissolved into a haze of grief and dread. James's uncle's house felt like a mausoleum, every room heavy with things left unsaid, the air steeped in a sadness that clung to the walls. James was a ghost in his own life. He paced without direction, stopped mid-sentence and forgot what he was saying, murmured warnings like a man with a fevered dream stitched into his skull.

Love tried to anchor him. She made tea he never drank. She brought food he didn't touch. She listened when he whispered fragments under his breath, fragments that scratched at the inside of her skull long after he stopped speaking.

"Should have seen it coming... the silence hides things..."

"Secrets rot people. They leak through the floorboards..."

She told herself it was grief talking. Shock. The mind cracking under weight it was never meant to carry, but the words burrowed deep.

His parents barely left his side. Eleanor clung to him in quiet desperation, while Arthur lingered in doorways, always watchful, always composed. One afternoon, Eleanor took Love's hand and held it tightly, as if afraid she might float away too.

"James needs you more than anyone. Please... stay close to him. Don't let him slip through."

Love nodded, unsure how to explain that she was slipping too.

Felix Sinclair's presence clung to her long after he was gone. He had spoken carefully, with just enough kindness, just enough distance. Nothing obvious. Nothing you could point to and call a mistake.

Still, a splinter lodged somewhere deep beneath her skin. A feeling she could not explain, only endure.

His name scratched faintly at her memory, a sound she could not place but could not seem to forget.

Somewhere in the hollow space between James's grief-strangled mutterings and the silence Felix left behind, something waited. Something she could not quite name but already feared.

◇◇◇◇◇

Back at Alexei's apartment, the world shrank until it felt airless. Everything was too polished, too precise, arranged like a scene meant to be admired but not touched. His words were soft, carefully chosen, shaped to soothe rather than stir. He asked about James, about Clara's funeral, about what she needed, offering his car, his time, his home without hesitation.

Love smiled when expected, nodded when appropriate. Her body stayed, but her mind was already somewhere else, measuring everything left unsaid. When he kissed her forehead with that aching gentleness, she forced herself not to recoil. The tenderness sat heavy against her skin, not comforting but hollow, like being wrapped in a blanket woven from broken promises.

In the silence he mistook for safety, she built her revolt.

She leaked fragments from copied files into activist networks. She sent anonymous tips to city regulators, each carefully timed to widen the cracks. She tampered with permit submissions, sowing just enough confusion to delay without drawing suspicion.

For a time, it steadied her. Every small sabotage became a prayer, a way to burn through the guilt she no longer knew how to confess.

Eventually even that thin sense of purpose began to rot.

One evening, after drifting through a hollow day at the station pretending to work, she returned to find Alexei waiting by the door. He had come back from Boston, his shirt rumpled, exhaustion tugging at the corners of his mouth.

He pulled her into his arms without a word, pressing his lips to her hair as if anchoring himself to something he could still believe in.

She let him.

Her hands moved on their own, circling his waist, drawing him closer. On the outside, she looked whole. Inside, she felt herself splitting down unseen seams.

"You look exhausted," he said, holding her with a gentleness that made her skin crawl.

She didn't have time to answer. A sharp pain twisted low in her stomach, sudden and deep enough to steal her breath. She pulled back, pressing a hand to her abdomen.

"Love?" He stepped closer, already reading the fear on her face. "What's wrong?"

"I'm fine," she said too quickly. "Just cramps. Starting my period, I think."

He tilted his head, confused. "Really? I thought... didn't you say you were feeling off a few weeks ago? That morning when you skipped breakfast?"

Her blood went cold.

A few weeks ago.

No. That was longer.

She smiled through her panic. "Everything's off lately. With James... and Clara... stress messes everything up."

She moved away before he could say more. Locked herself in the bathroom and stared at her reflection. Pale. Tired. Eyes too wide.

The dates clicked into place like bones snapping back into a broken shape.

She hadn't bled in nearly two months.

The nausea. The fatigue. The faintness. She had written it off. She had been too busy playing god to notice her body turning traitor beneath her.

Later that night, while Alexei slept peacefully beside her, she pulled on her coat and slipped from the apartment. The corner drugstore was bright and sharp, every fluorescent aisle exposing her. She grabbed the test and paid without looking the cashier in the eye.

She used the guest bathroom. Not the master. Not the one she sometimes showered in. She needed space, distance. The test felt heavier than it should. Her hands trembled as she followed the instructions, then set it down like it might explode.

She watched the timer on her phone.

One minute.

Two.

Three.

She turned it over. Stared. Refused to blink.

Two lines.

Clear. Solid. No room for interpretation.

Pregnant.

She mouthed the word but didn't say it aloud. Saying it aloud might make it true.

Her hands were shaking, but the rest of her was strangely still, like her body had given up trying to fight what her mind refused to accept. She'd spent the last few months hollowing herself out to make space for vengeance. Now something was trying to grow inside that hollowed space, and it made her feel... diseased. Not nurturing. Not motherly. Infected.

The test didn't blink. It didn't bargain. It just stared back at her from the counter, quiet and unflinching, as if it already understood exactly what she was and didn't need her permission to be right.

She pressed her palm to her stomach, moved by an impulse so raw it frightened her. It was not curiosity. It was not instinct. It was a desperate need to crush whatever had taken root before it could bloom into something she would never be able to erase. A lump rose thick in her throat and she swallowed hard, forcing the bitterness down, swallowing again when it clawed its way back up.

This could not be real. She refused it.

Not now. Not after everything.

Not with him.

The weight in her belly felt foreign, invasive, something curling through her veins that did not belong to her. It was not life. It was possession. It was a haunting taking shape inside her, threading itself into her bones, wearing the outline of Alexei's smile and carrying the silence that had once hollowed Ophelia's voice into nothing.

Nausea rose sharp and bitter and she stumbled to the sink, bracing herself hard against the porcelain as her body wretched against itself. No relief came, only the hollow retching of dry lungs and the sound of her own breath breaking in the tight, sterile air.

When she lifted her face to the mirror, she barely recognized what she saw. Her pupils were wide and wild. Her mouth had drained of color. Her eyes were smeared red with sleeplessness and something more dangerous brewing underneath, something raw that had not yet found a way to tear itself free.

She gripped the counter tighter, fighting the urge to smash her own reflection into dust, and whispered under her breath to no one.

She looked like a woman on the edge of a confession, or a breakdown, and neither option gave her any comfort.

Without thinking, she grabbed the test and flung it into the trash. It wasn't recklessness. It was fury. Disbelief. A desperate attempt to throw the moment away, to pretend it hadn't happened. This was stress, she told herself. It was a trick of hormones, a byproduct of grief, a false positive. The universe didn't have this twisted sense of humor.

She opened the medicine cabinet, slammed it shut, then opened it again with more force, scanning the shelves for some kind of reassurance—another test, an explanation, a label that could offer her reprieve. She checked the instructions, hoping for a loophole, a clause that would say stress skewed the results or mourning made the hormone levels lie. But the box said nothing. The box was merciless.

Still, she told herself the test was wrong. One test didn't mean anything. One line didn't mean a life. It could be a mistake. It had to be.

She rubbed her palms hard over her face, digging her fingernails into her cheeks, as if she could claw the thought out of her mind, as if pain could override reality. Then she reached into the trash with shaking hands, fished out the test, shoved it into a Ziploc bag, wrapped it tightly in a ball of tissues, and buried it at the very bottom of her backpack.

She didn't want it in the bathroom. She didn't want it in the trash. She didn't want it anywhere near her while she slept.

She didn't want it anywhere at all.

It wasn't real.

It wasn't.

She'd buy a new test. She'd take it. It would be negative. The world would right itself. She wasn't carrying his child. She wasn't that cursed.

Not real. Not real. Not real. She chanted it like a mantra hoping it would become her reality.

Chapter 24:

Two Lines

Love sat on the cold tile floor of the guest bathroom, knees drawn up to her chest, arms wrapped so tightly around herself it felt like she was trying to hold in the scream clawing its way up her throat. Her eyes burned, locked on the test stick in front of her.

Pregnant.

She hadn't kept track. Not really. There had been so much going on. James. Clara. Alexei's recovery. She was under stress. That threw cycles off. Hormones got weird. Maybe she was sick. Maybe it was a tumor or a cyst or something. Not this.

She stood with effort, legs shaky, and opened the bathroom door. She had to be sure. She had to get more tests.

Her keys were on the nightstand.

She could be back before Alexei noticed. He had been asleep when she slipped in here. Maybe he still was.

She grabbed her coat and shoes without bothering to fix her hair or wipe her face. Her reflection in the mirror was haunted, but she didn't care. She didn't feel real anyway.

The hallway was quiet. The apartment was too still.

She left like a shadow and didn't look back.

The pharmacy was bright and humming under too-harsh lights. She avoided the cashier's eyes, took three different brands again, and used the self-checkout this time. The bag crinkled too loud in her fist. She walked back slowly, nauseous, her feet barely touching the pavement. She didn't want to go back, but she didn't have anywhere else to go.

By the time she locked the door behind her, the panic was a live thing under her skin. She practically ran to the bathroom, locked the door, peeled off her coat, and ripped open the boxes like she was disarming a bomb. She took all three tests. Set them down. Waited.

The first one had shown a faint second line. The second, digital, had spelled it out in quiet, clinical certainty.

And the third... the third hadn't even hesitated. That pink line had flared into existence the moment urine hit the stick. Unapologetic. Unforgiving.

She stared at them like they were alien artifacts. Her fingers were white against her arms. Her breath came shallow and quick. She counted the seconds between inhales, between the tremors in her hands, between the growing need to run.

No.

It had to be wrong.

Love backed away from the counter like the tests might catch fire. Her heel hit the edge of the bathtub and she dropped to the floor with a thud, breath knocked from her lungs.

This time, the sob came out of her in a violent burst. She gasped once, then again, then screamed.

Not words. Just sound. Raw, feral, awful.

She hit the floor with her palm. Slapped the tile again. Pulled her hair. Rocked forward until her forehead touched the cold porcelain of the tub. Screamed again. Higher. Louder. Until her throat went raw and her voice cracked. She couldn't breathe. She couldn't stop.

The test boxes spilled from the sink.

One fell into her lap, mocking her with its branding. "Easy Read. Early Result. Clear Answer."

She threw it across the room.

The door burst open with a bang that rattled the hinges.

Alexei was half-dressed, barefoot, hair still mussed from sleep, eyes wide and unfocused as they scanned the room. His voice came sharp, frantic.

"Love?"

She didn't look up at first. She was curled on the bathroom floor, knees tucked to her chest, her arms wrapped around herself so tightly her nails had drawn crescent moons into her skin. Her breath came in short, panicked gasps. The test sticks lay scattered across the marble like evidence at a crime scene.

Alexei took a slow step forward.

"What happened?"

His gaze dropped to the floor, and the moment his eyes locked onto the three pregnancy tests, everything shifted.

The tension in the air changed.

A long breath escaped him, ragged but hopeful. He knelt beside her, reaching out.

"You're... are you pregnant?"

She didn't answer.

Her face snapped toward him like a puppet yanked by invisible strings.

The look in her eyes was not joy. Not surprise. Not even fear.

It was horror.

He froze mid-reach.

"Love?"

Then she screamed.

A sound tore out of her like her soul was being exorcised. High, guttural, unrelenting. She shoved herself away from him, crawling back until she slammed against the far wall. Her foot hit the trash can. It toppled. Empty packaging spilled. The second test skittered across the tile and hit the baseboard.

"No, no, no, this isn't....this can't be real," she gasped, her voice raw. "This isn't happening."

Alexei tried again to approach. "Love, it's okay. We can talk about this. It's a shock but we'll figure it out."

"Don't come near me!" she shrieked, grabbing the ceramic soap dish from the counter and hurling it at the floor near his feet. It shattered.

He flinched, stunned.

"What are you doing?" His voice pitched higher, confused now, concern melting into fear. "What's wrong?"

Her hands raked through her hair, nails catching. She was breathing too fast. Hyperventilating. A sob burst from her lips. Then another. She tried to stand and stumbled. Her hand caught the edge of the sink. The mirror tilted under her weight.

"This is a nightmare," she whispered, eyes wild. "This is punishment. This is some twisted, sick joke from the universe."

She looked at him then, really looked at him, and recoiled like she'd seen something monstrous.

Alexei reached out again, slowly this time, like she was a skittish animal. "Please, Love. You're scaring me. You're not okay. Talk to me. What's happening?"

"You!" she cried, voice splintering. "It's you!"

That stopped him.

"What about me?"

"You ruined everything," she spat. "Everything you touch turns to rot. It spreads. It infects. And now it's inside me.." Her voice cracked mid-word. "I can't breathe."

He stepped forward, panic flashing in his eyes.

She lashed out, swinging the plastic cup from the sink. Water splashed across the counter and soaked the edge of the rug. Her foot slipped. She caught herself on the doorframe.

He didn't know whether to move closer or back away.

"I'm going to be sick," she choked out, clutching her stomach. "I'm going to throw up. Or claw it out. Or drown it. I don't know."

His face went pale.

"Love, you're not making sense. Please. Sit down. Let me get you help. Let me get you water. You need to breathe."

She collapsed against the wall, fingers curled in her hair, sobbing now in great, shuddering waves. "Three tests. Three. I did them all. I bought them like a coward, snuck out while you were sleeping. Like some thief in my own body."

She laughed then. A horrible, wet, hysterical sound.

"And the worst part is you look happy. You actually look happy."

"Of course I am," Alexei said, eyes wide. "I thought... I thought it was good news."

That did it.

She lunged toward the counter and swept the rest of the tests into the sink with one frantic motion, sending them clattering like broken bones. "Do I look like someone with good news, Alexei?"

"Please stop," he whispered, voice cracking.

She gripped the edge of the sink, her shoulders rising and falling with each tortured breath. Her reflection stared back at her. A ghost. A monster. A girl already in the process of being consumed.

When she spoke again, her voice was quiet. Hollow.

"Don't."

The word stopped him cold.

"I need space," she said. Her voice was shaking. "Just....don't talk to me. Don't touch me. Don't pretend to fix this."

Then she turned and walked out, barefoot, past the shards, past him, down the hall and into the guest room.

She closed the door gently, locked it, and slid down the back, curling into herself in the silence.

Behind her closed lids, the word glowed in the dark like a curse.

Pregnant.

Chapter 25:

Oscar-worthy

The silence after her breakdown rang louder than the screams. Morning light spilled across the apartment in soft gold, brushing against the broken pieces of last night — the upturned glass, the smeared tear tracks on the marble floor, the ghost of her voice still echoing in the walls. Love had curled into herself on the edge of the guest bed, awake all night, eyes burning. Her body ached, her throat raw, but her mind moved with ruthless clarity.

She had lost control. Let the truth boil too close to the surface. And he had seen it — the teeth, the venom. Her reaction was nuclear. There was no undoing the detonation, but she could still sift through the ashes and build the illusion back stronger. If she didn't, he would know. And if he knew... everything would fall apart.

When Alexei knocked gently on the bedroom door, she forced herself to sit upright. He stepped inside slowly, like approaching a wounded animal, his expression cautious but open. Love looked at him and felt nothing. No fear, no warmth. Only calculation. This was the man she had accused with her body, even if the words hadn't crossed her lips. She'd thrown glass, sobbed like she was haunted, screamed at him like she was grieving a ghost — and in many ways, she was.

"I wanted to give you space," he said quietly, "but I needed to know if you're alright." He paused. "I didn't mean to make you feel cornered last night."

Her lips trembled. She dropped her gaze. A performance was only as good as its stakes, and this one had to be Oscar-worthy.

"I broke a little," she whispered, voice hoarse. "I—I didn't even recognize myself."

He sat across from her but didn't reach for her. He was giving her control, waiting.

"I didn't want it to happen like that," she said, tears collecting again. "I took three tests, Alexei. And each one... it just made it more real. And I got scared. Not because of you. But because of me."

She blinked slowly, letting tears fall like she wasn't even trying to stop them.

"I haven't been okay. Not really. Not since Ophelia. I've been pretending I'm functional, but I'm not. I've been surviving on caffeine and compartmentalization. I forgot how to feel things at the right volume. It all comes out wrong."

Alexei moved a little closer.

"You didn't do anything wrong," she added quickly, voice cracking. "You were kind. You were gentle. And I just... lashed out. Because for a moment, you looked happy. Like... really happy. And I couldn't understand it. I envied it. I hated how safe you felt. And I was terrified. Because I know I can't give that back to you."

Alexei finally reached for her hand. "You don't have to give me anything but yourself."

She nodded, slowly, biting her lip, like she was trying to believe him.

"I'm sorry I said all those horrible things. I was scared. Not of you. Of what this means."

He pulled her into a tentative embrace. She let herself sink into him like a girl too exhausted to stand on her own.

"I don't want to be a monster," she whispered against his chest.

"You're not."

Oh, but she was. The worst part was, she was getting very good at pretending she wasn't.

IN THE FOLLOWING DAYS, Love crafted her escape plan with surgical precision. She confirmed her appointment for Tuesday in a city several hours away and spun the perfect alibi: a long-overdue sleepover with Layla. The text she sent her best friend was layered with guilt, charm, and just the right hint of emotional distress.

"Layla. I've been the worst friend and I hate myself for it. Everything's falling apart with James, and now... things with Alexei are spiraling too. I just need one night to breathe. Please say I can come over Tuesday. I'll bring snacks and we can roast the new season of that trash dating show."

Layla replied within minutes.

"Babe. Always. Come decompress. I'll pick the trashiest show - wigs flying and everything."

Love forced a laugh. The irony was cruel. She hated how easy it was to lie now.

The next move was Felix.

He haunted her thoughts more than she wanted to admit. There was something about his presence — not just the eerie calm, but the sense of detachment, the way he took in a room like someone who had been trained to find the exits before sitting down. He was dangerous, but danger, when used properly, was leverage.

She texted him under the guise of gratitude, making sure it read like an olive branch, not a red flag.

"Hi Felix. Thank you again for the resources you shared. James's parents are finally speaking to someone. Would love to thank you in person. Coffee?"

He responded almost immediately.

"Tomorrow. 4pm. Maison Vert. Discretion guaranteed."

Discretion guaranteed

That made her stomach twist. Either he had enemies, or he was one.

◈ ⚓ ◈ ⚓ ◈

Maison Vert smelled faintly of cinnamon bark and old paper, the kind of café where whispered conversations were expected, not encouraged. Love slipped inside and immediately found him tucked into the corner near the frosted windows, where the late afternoon light slanted in thin, pale ribbons.

Felix rose smoothly as she approached, adjusting the sleeve of his charcoal coat with the unthinking grace of someone raised among men who never rushed for anything.

"Ms. Godfrey," he said, voice low and perfectly modulated.

"Felix," she returned, matching his poise.

They spoke first of James. Of Clara. Of grief and how it threads itself through a family, weaving silence between words that once flowed easily. Felix listened more than he spoke, hands folded lightly around his espresso cup, posture relaxed but never careless.

It wasn't until the conversation softened into quieter currents that Love shifted the tide.

"Layla mentioned," she said carefully, "that your family is connected to the estate where the party was held...the one James' uncle also uses for social events."

Felix's mouth curved into something that wasn't quite a smile. It was softer than that.

"Yes," he said, "our families have managed different properties together for years. Old ties. Old favors."

Love toyed with the edge of her napkin, keeping her tone even.

"I think I saw Alexei there that night too."

At the mention of his name, Felix's eyes, a shade too pale to ever seem fully warm, flickered. Not a reaction, not a tell, but something like the brief drawing of a curtain in a house you didn't realize was being watched.

"Yes," he said, and for the first time, there was a thread of something almost personal in his voice.

"Our families have crossed paths often. Especially in more... private circles."

He said it like an offhand observation, a simple fact, but it slid under Love's skin and lodged there.

She offered a small, polite nod as if none of it mattered.

Felix, as if sensing the weight his words had dropped between them, took a sip of his espresso and continued casually,

"Men like Alexei tend to leave impressions. Even when they don't intend to."

The statement was neutral. Perfectly neutral. Yet it left the tiniest crack in the wall of her mind, a hairline fracture she could feel widening even as she smiled and murmured something noncommittal in response.

The conversation drifted after that, dissolving back into polite remarks about travel, weather, familiar obligations. Felix never pressed. Never lingered too long on anything sharp. He moved through the interaction the way an old spy moves through a crowd — leaving no footprints, no fingerprints, only the faint suggestion that he had been there at all.

When he rose to leave, he buttoned his coat with the same slow, meticulous ease he had arrived with.

"If you ever need perspective," he said, voice as polite as a closing door, "sometimes it helps to step outside the picture you're inside of."

Love watched him go, the soft hush of his departure blending into the background noise of clinking cups and murmured conversation.

She stayed seated, her coffee long cold, her mind already pulling at the seam he had left behind....

A faint and crawling sense that somewhere in the architecture of her life, another blueprint was unfolding. One she hadn't drawn.

Chapter 26:

S tockholm Syndrome?

The drive south felt like a slow glide through purgatory. Morning light crept over the horizon in pale, colorless streaks, bleeding into the car interior, washing everything in gray. Love gripped the steering wheel tightly, eyes fixed ahead, ignoring the ache deep in her lower abdomen and the hollow flutter in her chest. Alexei had still been sleeping when she left, arms sprawled, face soft with sleep. She had leaned in, murmured something quiet and fragile. "Going to Layla's. Be back tomorrow." He kissed her temple and mumbled, "Take care of yourself, moya lyubov."

The way her throat tightened at that nearly made her wreck the car.

The clinic sat hidden in a sleepy downtown block of a neighboring city, the kind of place designed to look like a dentist's office. Neutral walls. Frosted glass windows. A sliding door that swallowed you like a secret.

She checked in under her real name. A fake one would be harder to explain later, riskier. Besides, she wasn't hiding from the world. She was just choosing what part of it to destroy.

The waiting room was too quiet. Muted. No one looked at each other. It wasn't shame. It was something colder. Something more exhausted. When the nurse called her name, it sounded like a dare.

The procedure was efficient. Clean. The nurse spoke in a soft, practiced voice as she explained each step, her tone coated in sterile empathy. Love didn't respond. She lay still, eyes fixed on the water stain spreading like a bruise across the ceiling tile. One small brown bloom just beside the light. She clung to it, let it anchor her, while the machine hummed beside her and a strange pressure pulled through her core. It wasn't pain. Pain might have felt personal. This felt mechanical—a system flushing itself, methodically erasing something once alive.

She didn't cry. Not then. Not afterward, when she sat in recovery sipping cold apple juice from a paper cup that had already softened from how tightly she held it. What she felt wasn't grief, nor relief. It was something more final. A scorched earth feeling. She had uprooted something, left nothing but ash in its place.

When she drove away, the silence inside the car felt earned. She didn't reach for the radio. Didn't need distraction. She didn't head to Layla's like she'd said she might. Instead, she veered off onto an old roadside rest area, parking beneath the skeleton of a flickering lamp. The car faced a patch of scrub trees, half-dead and leaning, just like she felt. For a long time she didn't move. Her forehead rested against the steering wheel, breath shallow, body trembling. The tears still didn't come.

This wasn't numbness. It was absence. Not a frozen feeling, but an excavation. There was nothing left inside her to thaw.

Eventually, she opened the trunk and pulled out her burner laptop, setting it on the passenger seat as it powered on with a tired hum. Her fingers moved with a kind of mechanical discipline, not from focus but from memory. Routine.

The Swiss blog had posted again, citing "renewed attention" on offshore banking irregularities linked to Chervyakov Holdings. Another article on the environmental site noted a quiet investigation into the Mill Zone development after a rise in community complaints. The small explosions she had planted were beginning to detonate—slow, subtle, effective.

Still, it wasn't enough.

She opened her encrypted inbox and drafted two new messages. The first was to an investor she remembered from the gala, someone who had lingered too long in Alexei's orbit. Her tone was just right—casual concern laced with unspoken warning, hinting at "emotional instability" and "unreliable political ties." The second email was colder, sharper, addressed to an executive deep within his father's inner circle. It offered no proof, only implication. A whisper of distraction. A suggestion of recklessness. A few lines insinuating that Alexei's local involvement might endanger larger assets.

She didn't embellish. She didn't overexplain. Just poison, dripped carefully between the lines.

Then she leaned back in the seat, watching her reflection in the darkened window. Her own face looked unfamiliar. Not haunted, but stripped. Like someone who had nothing left to give, and too much still to do.

◈ ◈❀◈❀◈❀◈

By the time she arrived at Layla's, she had practiced her smile to perfection.

Layla opened the door in fuzzy socks and a vintage band tee that had seen too many heartbreaks. Her curls were in a pineapple bun, glitter still stubbornly clinging to her cheekbones like a protest. She didn't ask questions. Just pulled Love into the kind of hug that said I've got you, no matter how bad it is."

Love sank into the familiar cushions of the sofa like someone returning from war.

"How are you?" Layla asked, sitting across from her, already pouring wine. "And don't give me that 'I'm fine' crap."

Love laughed softly. It was almost genuine. "I'm just tired, Lay. Everything's been so... heavy. James, Clara, work... and then Alexei on top of it all."

Layla handed her a glass. "Right. The enigmatic billionaire boyfriend. James said you were back in deep with him."

Love gave a small nod, staring into her wine. "Yeah. After the accident, I felt like I owed him something. He was vulnerable. I don't know, maybe I was too. It just... happened."

Layla raised a brow. "That doesn't sound very romantic."

Love forced a smile. "It's complicated. He's... kind. And intense. Protective. But there's always this fog around him. Like I'm standing outside a locked room."

Layla frowned. "Sounds exhausting. You sure it's not Stockholm Syndrome?"

Love let out a weak laugh. "That would be fitting, wouldn't it?" She paused, lowering her voice. "He doesn't know how to be soft unless he's hurting. That's the only time I see him clearly."

Layla blinked. "That's really dark."

Love shrugged. "That's how it feels."

While Layla ordered dinner, Love stepped into the bathroom, splashing cold water on her face. The woman in the mirror looked composed. But her eyes were flat. Hungerless. She was slipping too far into the mask. She touched her stomach. Flat now. Empty. He'll never know.

Her phone buzzed. A message from Alexei.

My Love, Forgive the intrusion. I know you're with Layla tonight, but I just wanted you to know how proud I am of you. How much I love you. Thinking about you and the baby. Always.

She stared at the screen for a long time.

The baby.

She typed a soft reply. Something gentle. Something he'd believe.

Then, for just a second, her hand trembled.

✪✪✪✪✪✪✪✪✪✪✪✪✪✪✪✪✪✪✪✪✪

Chapter 27:

Some Debts Are Paid In Silence

Love returned to Alexei's apartment from her clandestine clinic appointment feeling like a phantom limb—fully functional, but hollow at the center. She let herself melt into the role of the recovering girlfriend, the soft-spoken woman stunned by unexpected news, one who now clung to the man she had every intention of unmaking. She gave him everything he expected: downcast eyes, a tired smile, hands that trembled a little too perfectly. She apologized for being distant, for needing time. She said she felt better now. She let him kiss her forehead and tuck a blanket around her. She pretended it helped.

His tenderness was unbearable.

She hated mirrors now. They showed her a body that still remembered him. Curvy hips. A softness that once felt like warmth but now felt like evidence. Her copper hair clung to her cheeks, damp with sweat and fury.

The effects of her sabotage—most recently, the forged memo questioning the Brunswick Mill project's viability—had begun to ripple outward. She watched it from inside the safe cocoon of his trust, quiet and alert while his world slowly began to fracture. His frustration surfaced in increasingly sharp bursts. He paced more. He muttered, cursed under his breath. Video calls ran late into the night, full of terse language she didn't understand but could read in tone.

 ❦ ◈ ❦❦ ◈ ❦❦ ◈ ❦

"Something's wrong," he said one evening, dropping heavily onto the couch beside her. His hands rubbed his face, the exhaustion evident in every movement. "There's a leak. Someone is feeding investors false information.

They're pulling back, freezing commitments, questioning everything. The project's hemorrhaging confidence."

Love curled closer, her hand resting gently on his shoulder. "What kind of information?"

"Highly specific financials. Staged delays. Permitting concerns I've already addressed. It's calculated. And whoever's doing it... they're surgical about it."

She murmured something sympathetic and pressed her face into his shirt, breathing in the scent of the man she was unraveling. It smelled like clean cotton and chaos.

Alexei didn't suspect her—of that, she was certain. His paranoia was directed elsewhere, his trust in her maddeningly intact. He spoke of interference, of sabotage, of people from the periphery with unknown motives. "It's deliberate," he told her, eyes bloodshot from a sleepless night. "Like someone's trying to cut out the floor beneath me without ever touching me."

He started sleeping less. Or not at all. She'd hear him moving around in the early hours, quiet, frantic, watching the city lights from the window like they held answers. The shadows under his eyes deepened. One morning, he stood in the kitchen gripping a mug with white-knuckled fingers, staring through her like he wasn't entirely sure she was real.

"I can't afford to slip," he said suddenly. "Not now. I've worked too hard to get out from under... everything."

She touched his hand, feigning concern. "You're not slipping."

Oh, but he was....and it was working.

James had faded from view. He attended grief counseling when prompted. He responded to messages when pressed. But the vibrant anger, the cryptic warnings—those had vanished. Now he just existed, like a man waiting for something to end. Love had tried, in passing, to ask about Clara's last weeks, about Felix, about anything that could tie the chaos together. But James only blinked at her, hollowed out and unreachable.

That suited her. Silence was easier than conscience.

Still, there were pieces missing. Felix lingered in her mind—not just his calculated presence, but the way he seemed to circle the narrative without fully entering it. He had been helpful, cautious, vague. He had alluded to shadows. She needed more. Something to confirm what she already believed.

She reached out again, texting from her regular phone this time.

"Would love to follow up on our last conversation. Some of what you said stuck with me. Could use more context if you're open to it."

Felix responded within an hour.

Same café. Same quiet corner.

The rain tapped at the windows in a slow, persistent rhythm, filling the quiet between them. Felix sat already waiting, the faintest shadow of amusement in his eyes as she slid into the booth across from him.

Love didn't waste time. She wrapped her hands around the lukewarm coffee cup and leaned in slightly, voice low.

"The last time we met, you mentioned ... that your world and Alexei's overlapped," she said. "Was it ever more than passing acquaintance?"

Felix's smile was faint, the kind meant to politely deflect without outright lying.

"Our families shared investments. Certain social circles. Real estate, mostly."

Love studied him for a beat longer than necessary, chewing the inside of her cheek.

"I'm not asking to pry," she said carefully. "It's just... I'm involved with him now. More than involved. And sometimes I feel like there are things he won't, or can't say."

Felix tilted his head slightly, the movement subtle, birdlike. For a moment, it seemed like he might brush the question aside.

Then he spoke, slow and deliberate.

"Men like Alexei... carry things differently. Burdens do not sit on their shoulders. They burrow deeper. Hidden places."

Love's throat tightened. She kept her expression neutral, but the words prickled under her skin.

"I'm worried about him," she admitted quietly. "There's so much I don't know. No one else seems to know his world. His past. It feels like standing in a house full of locked doors."

Felix's eyes darkened, but he smiled — a thin, mirthless thing.

"You should be careful which doors you try to open," he said. "Some houses were built on burial grounds."

Love swallowed hard. Her hand tightened around the coffee cup.

"I'm not trying to hurt him," she said. "I just want to understand."

Felix's gaze sharpened, almost pitying.

"Understanding is a blade, Ms. Godfrey. Once drawn, it cuts both ways."

She hesitated, but pressed further, voice softer now.

"Was there ever... anything worse? Anything dangerous?"

For a long moment, Felix just watched her, the weight of some private memory making his silence stretch unbearably thin.

Finally, he spoke, almost as if reciting a fable to a child.

"There were times," he said, "when Alexei moved too quickly. Burned too many bridges. Made too many promises he could not keep. Some debts are paid in silence. Others... collect interest."

Love's skin prickled.

Felix shrugged lightly, like a man tossing away the last scrap of conscience.

"But perhaps you will be different," he said. "Perhaps he will leave his ghosts behind for you."

He rose then, gathering his coat with methodical grace. His movement wasn't hurried, but it carried a kind of finality, as though the conversation had been neatly folded and placed into some pocket of his mind for later use.

Before he turned away completely, he glanced back over his shoulder, his voice low and smooth.

"Just remember," he said. "Not all ruins are abandoned by accident."

Then he left, the door swinging shut behind him with a whisper.

Love remained at the table, coffee cold and untouched, the seat across from her still faintly warm, as if he had only slipped into the mist outside and might reappear if she waited long enough.

She did not wait.

She gathered herself slowly, mechanically, stepping back into the night without a backward glance — but feeling, somehow, that she had crossed another threshold she would not return from.

✧ ✧ ✧

Her hands trembled as she opened the car door, the chill of the night sinking into her skin. She gripped the wheel harder than necessary on the drive home, the lines of the road blurring into one long, empty stretch.

By the time she stepped into the apartment, the world outside no longer mattered.

Alexei was asleep on the couch, half-dressed, one arm slung carelessly over his chest. The television flickered muted colors across his face. He looked peaceful. Untouched.

She hated him for it.

Love moved quietly through the living room, pausing just long enough to watch his chest rise and fall with every untroubled breath. Then she slipped into the kitchen, poured herself a glass of water, and leaned against the counter, the cold edge biting into her spine.

There was no grief left. No fear. No rage.

Only calculation.

The mask slid into place without effort, seamless and convincing. The performance would hold. It had to, but beneath it, something colder had begun to grow, sharp and irreversible.

Chapter 28 - Part 1:

Tonight, We Turn Off The World.

The acquisition of the handgun did not ignite her. It extinguished her. Somewhere deep in her chest, where fear used to pulse, there was only stillness now. The life she had built, the body she inhabited, the man she once thought she could save — none of it belonged to her anymore.

She moved through Alexei's apartment like a ghost who knew she was haunting herself. She kissed his shoulder, brewed his coffee, smiled in the softest ways, the ones he would not question. Every movement was clean. Every lie wrapped in tenderness he never thought to doubt.

Meanwhile, Alexei frayed at the edges, and then he frayed deeper. The funding for Brunswick disappeared into silence. Swiss regulators reopened the doors he had thought were sealed. His father no longer offered advice, only clipped orders delivered like verdicts. Their conversations grew shorter. Sharper. Somewhere between one call and the next, the approval Alexei had spent his life chasing was gone.

The apartment felt like a house abandoned mid-sentence. The papers no longer scattered with urgency. The late-night calls fell silent. The windows turned blank, reflecting nothing but the wreckage he refused to name.

He sat motionless for hours now, tracing patterns across invisible maps only he could see. No pacing. No planning. Just the slow, inevitable waiting of a man who understood that his own empire had begun to rot beneath him.

Love watched it all. She played the part beautifully. She touched his hand when he needed it. She offered comfort when he faltered. She kissed him goodnight like a prayer he was too far gone to answer.

Inside her, something colder bloomed, cutting sharper each day.

She had not simply stopped loving him. She had outlived the part of herself that ever could.

◇ ✧ ◇ ✧ ◇

"Someone is trying to dismantle everything," he murmured to himself after hanging up with his legal counsel, who'd used the word 'suspicious' three times in a row. "No one gets this close to a collapse unless they know where the soft spots are."

He stood barefoot in the kitchen, disheveled in a button-down he hadn't ironed, eyes red from another sleepless night. Love sat on a stool across from him, sipping warm tea like she hadn't been the one whispering poison into every weak seam of his empire.

"I'm doing everything I can," he said quietly, almost to himself. "The due diligence reports were airtight. I kept everything clean after the Eastern Bloc project. This doesn't make sense unless someone's rewriting the story."

"Maybe someone is," Love offered gently, crossing one leg over the other, casual. "Or maybe someone's... afraid of your potential." She made her voice soft, concerned. "People act irrationally when they feel threatened."

He looked at her for a long time then, his eyes hollow. "My father thinks I've gone soft. Says I'm distracted by... things." He didn't say you, but it hung there. "He told me if I can't salvage the Mill Zone, he's pulling the entire North American delegation and reassigning it to Zurich. To Viktor."

She blinked. "Who's Viktor?"

"Exactly," he said bitterly. "Some green technocrat who's never seen a failed audit or fought a zoning board with pitchforks. But he speaks five languages and doesn't sleep with 'liabilities.'"

Love tilted her head. "So now you're a liability?"

He gave a laugh that wasn't a laugh. "To him? Probably. I went off-script. I started building a life."

He meant her. The phantom baby. The dinners. The comfort. He thought he'd built something safe around them.

She stood up and walked to him, pressed a kiss to his temple. "You're going to get through this. They'll see what they've got in you." She let the lie taste sweet in her mouth before swallowing it whole. "I believe in you."

It was a script. One she'd written herself.

He wrapped his arms around her, burying his face in her shoulder like a man clinging to the last raft of his wrecked ship. Love held him, not tightly, but firmly. She didn't console him. She contained him. She was the perimeter. She was the storm.

❖ ❖ ✦ ❖ ❖ ❖ ❖ ✦ ❖ ❖

The next few days deepened the cracks in ways silence never could. His assistant, nervous and tight-lipped, forwarded him a chain of emails that began at an anonymous tip line and wound its way through bureaucratic whispers until it reached his inbox. The message implied a concern—"emotional instability" in Alexei's handling of city development permits. A day later, one of his more cautious investors requested his most recent psychological clearance report. Psychological clearance. Love had nearly laughed when she overheard it. She had invented the phrasing herself late one night, fingers curled around his old corporate statements, threading just enough precision into the lie to sound clinical—just enough venom to be fatal.

Alexei stopped shaving. Then, without announcement, he stopped sleeping in the bed. For two nights, he collapsed fully clothed on the couch, a half-finished glass of scotch at his side, the television on mute while news tickers flashed across his face like the last rites of a dying empire. Love tucked a blanket over him each time, her hands careful, her gaze neutral. Like preparing a body for burial. She kissed his hairline once. Not out of fondness. Out of ritual.

She visited her family in the midst of it all, keeping the illusion of normalcy stitched together with practiced smiles and mumbled reassurances. Her mother asked about prenatal vitamins. Her father asked if she was eating enough. Her brother asked whether Alexei knew where the brakes were on this runaway relationship. They looked at her the way you look at someone still sipping tea in a burning house, unwilling to leave.

❖ ❖ ❖

When she got back home, Alexei didn't ask where she had been. He only asked if she could make him coffee. He drank it slowly, hands cupped around the mug like he was mourning the last warmth in the world. His voice cracked when he said, "You're the only thing I've done right this year."

For a moment, something in Love flinched. Not guilt. Not regret. Something quieter, harder to name. A pull in her chest, like gravity, like the memory of trust. It wasn't forgiveness. But it was close. A breath away from the girl she used to be, the one who might've believed in accidents, in errors made by good men. But that girl had burned, and the ash wasn't enough to start again.

She kissed his forehead. Her hand brushed his jaw. "Tonight," she murmured, "we turn off the world."

The smile she gave him was soft, almost reverent. A memory of something she used to mean.

Chapter 28 - Part II:

Baby Names

That evening unfolded with a gentleness that felt rehearsed. Alexei lit the candles himself, adjusting the wicks with deliberate care, ensuring the flames stood tall but calm. The room glowed with an intimacy that didn't feel earned—it felt borrowed. Like a final act set on a stage built for someone else's happy ending. He even changed clothes, choosing a crisp white shirt with the sleeves rolled to the elbow, invoking a version of himself she hadn't seen in weeks. The man who charmed his way into her life, not the one unraveling in silence.

Love wore an oversized hoodie and grey leggings, her hair pulled back in a loose braid, her face bare of anything but the weight of intention. She looked like comfort. Like vulnerability. Like someone who still needed her partner. The illusion was nearly perfect.

The Thai food arrived just after eight. They ate cross-legged on the couch, digging into cartons with chopsticks, a muted old film playing in the background. A hum of distant dialogue filled the spaces they didn't.

Alexei turned to her halfway through the meal, chopsticks resting against the side of his plate. His voice was soft, almost hesitant. "Thank you," he said, eyes searching her face. "For sticking with me through all this. I know I haven't been easy lately."

Love smiled gently, placing a hand over his. "We're in this together, remember?"

He looked at her hand, then at her face. His gaze held that old intensity, the one that used to make her blush.

"I keep thinking," he said quietly, "about what it'll be like. When we're through this. When things are stable. When we're... parents."

There it was. The word. *Parents.*

Love's stomach turned, but she nodded. "It'll be... different," she said, and for once the ambiguity was honest.

Alexei took a long sip of wine, then leaned back into the cushions, staring up at the ceiling. "Have you thought about names yet?"

She laughed, too quickly, too loud. "What?"

"For the baby," he said, smiling. "I know it's early, but it's been on my mind. I keep running through them in my head like I'm naming a ship. Something strong, something meaningful."

"Oh God," Love said, shaking her head. "You're going to pick something dramatic, aren't you?"

"Only if you let me," he teased. "But I've been thinking. If it's a boy... Nikolai? Or Julian, maybe. Julian Chervyakov has a nice ring to it."

Love forced a chuckle, twirling a noodle around her chopstick. "Julian sounds like someone who owns silk pajamas and corrects your grammar mid-argument."

"Exactly," he grinned. "Classy."

She played along, watching him closely, waiting for the turn.

"And if it's a girl?"

He took a beat, then said, "Ekaterina? Or maybe something bolder. Agrippina."

Love snorted. "If you think I'm naming our child Agrippina Chervyakov, you've officially lost—"

She stopped.

It slammed into her like a freight train. Our child. Our.

The air changed. Her voice had sharpened with genuine disbelief, and it echoed in the room with too much weight. Alexei blinked. "Lost...?"

Love froze. Her chopsticks were suspended mid-air. Her breath caught.

"No, I—sorry," she said quickly, waving her hand. " I just—my God, that name."

Alexei didn't look away. "Lost what, Love?"

Her heart hammered against her ribs. "Your mind. I meant to say your mind. I'm tired," she muttered, rising from the couch. "Too tired for baby name debates."

"Love," he said again, quietly now, watching her cross to the kitchen with her back too straight, her shoulders too stiff. "I was joking. Agrippina is... historically absurd. I didn't think you'd actually react that strongly."

"Well I did," she said too fast, rinsing her hands at the sink that didn't need rinsing. "It's a weird name. It sounds like a disease."

Alexei stood, wine glass in hand, and moved toward her slowly. "You said our child. Then you stopped like you forgot who we are."

She turned to him, smiling too brightly. "Can we not psychoanalyze my dinner table meltdown? I'm not exactly emotionally stable right now."

"I know you," he said. "And that... that wasn't just a meltdown."

The silence between them was no longer warm. It was clinical. Observational.

Love moved back toward the couch and sat down, cross-legged again, forcing her breath to steady. "You're right," she said softly. "I overreacted. I just... it's been a lot. Everything with James, the hormones, the stress. Sometimes it just... leaks out sideways."

He joined her again, the pause between them stretching like fabric about to tear. He looked at her, brow creased in something that wasn't quite suspicion—just confusion. Deep and gnawing.

"I'm sorry," she whispered, letting her voice break slightly. "I'm just mentally and physically exhausted."

Alexei's expression softened, like a man who desperately wanted the explanation to be enough. He took her hand again, threading their fingers together. "You don't have to be perfect. Not for me. Just talk to me, okay?"

Love nodded. "I will."

She kissed his cheek, lingering there a moment too long.

He sighed, leaning back again, eyes closed. "I'll never pick another baby name without your full approval," he murmured.

She smiled without smiling.

When he fell asleep that night, his head resting against her thigh, she stared at the ceiling and thought about how easily love became rot. Not all at once. Just drip by drip. A name. A joke. A single syllable with too much weight.

Tomorrow. It would be tomorrow.

Because now he was slipping through her fingers, and if she didn't act soon, she might slip with him.

Chapter 29 - Part 1:

O*phelia*
The apartment felt too clean. Too deliberate. As if someone had pressed pause on a life halfway lived and carefully polished the remains. The lights were dimmed to a soft amber haze. The table had been set, but the wine remained corked. The food sat untouched. A candle flickered quietly beside a folded napkin, casting fragile shadows across the room.

Love sat curled into the far corner of the couch, one leg tucked beneath her, the other twitching faintly. She wasn't seated for comfort—she'd chosen that spot for the vantage point. From here, she could see the door. The window. Him.

Across from her, Alexei lounged in a posture that betrayed exhaustion more than ease. One leg bent, arm draped casually over the back of the sofa, glass in hand. He was mid-story—something about Zurich, boardroom politics, people with expensive shoes and no conscience. His voice was warm, steady, unguarded in that rare way that happened only behind closed doors.

But Love wasn't listening. Not really.

Every word he spoke slid past her like static. She nodded at the right moments. Let a smile ghost her lips when his tone asked for one. But her mind had drifted—somewhere deeper. Somewhere colder. The intimacy he offered now felt like a betrayal. A bedtime story told after the murder scene had been scrubbed clean.

He didn't know he was speaking to a girl made of wires and knives.

He took another sip of wine. "You're quiet tonight," he said softly, glancing at her over the rim of the glass. A faint smile pulled at his lips. "Still thinking about names?"

Love blinked slowly. That question—it was like the sound of ice cracking beneath her feet.

She smiled, barely. "Something like that."

He chuckled gently. "I can't stop picturing a little girl with your eyes. Fierce. Beautiful. Completely terrifying."

Her hands tightened beneath the blanket.

He turned toward her fully, his voice playful now, reaching across the stillness between them like he was testing a bridge. "Alright. Serious question. What if it's a boy and you still refuse to name him Igor? I feel like that's something we should settle before the hospital paperwork."

She let out a small breath, the kind that might've once been a laugh.

"And what if it's a girl?" he continued, eyes brightening. "What about Algebrina? Dramatic. Regal. Definitely traumatizing enough to give her character."

Something broke.

The word hung in the air—*Algebrina*—absurd, ridiculous, but it twisted in her gut like a hook. Her expression cracked open into something disbelieving. Not amusement. Not offense.

Rage.

She sat up abruptly, the blanket sliding off her legs in a ripple. "Algebrina?" she repeated, and her voice cut like glass.

Alexei blinked. "It's a joke, lyubov."

She stared at him, breath suddenly shallow. "No, you're serious. You're sitting there trying to name a child you don't deserve."

His brow furrowed. "What?"

"Do I look like someone who would sentence a child to playground exile?"

He stared, unsure whether to laugh or apologize. But she wasn't laughing. The energy in the room had changed, slamming into something sharp and invisible. She stood, pacing toward the window. Her hands trembled. Her voice didn't.

"Do you ever think about what comes after?" she asked without turning around. "About what you're building? Or do you just bulldoze everything in your way and call it legacy?"

Alexei rose slowly, the ease gone from his posture. "Love... what's going on?"

She turned back to him, her gaze steady now. Fixed. "Ophelia."

His entire body stilled. The name cracked through the room like a whip. He froze, eyes wide, mouth parting slightly as if he'd been struck.

She took a step forward, the weight of it final.

"You knew her."

Chapter 29 - Part II:

Burning Church

Alexei rose slowly, like a man standing in a burning church, unsure whether to run or kneel. His body moved first, instinctual, confused. His eyes trailed behind, uncomprehending. He planted his weight on his heels, like the floor had tilted beneath him—like he'd just stepped onto the edge of a grave he didn't know he dug.

"Love..." Her name cracked from his lips. Not soft. Not tender. Scared. A single word, but it staggered with the weight of everything unraveling inside him. "Why would you say her name like that?"

She didn't blink.

Because blinking was for the living.

"Because you knew her," she said. The syllables landed like footsteps in a tomb. Calm. Final.

"What?" His brow creased, voice cracking on the edges. "No—I didn't—"

"Don't lie to me," she breathed, and it was almost gentle, but the gentleness was the kind that came before an execution.

Alexei stilled. Not out of defiance, but dread.

"I'm not...Love, I don't even know what you're talking about."

"You used her words." Her eyes were twin embers, hollowed by grief, lit by rage. "You said 'catch moonlight in a jar.' That wasn't yours to say."

He flinched.

Subtle. But not subtle enough.

She took a step forward, slow and measured, like every inch brought her closer to the truth she couldn't unsee.

"You said it like it meant something between us. Like it belonged to us. But it didn't. It was hers. And now she's dead."

His hands lifted, palms open, but he wasn't defending himself—he was surrendering to a war he didn't understand. "I didn't know..."

"Yes, you did." Her voice cracked—not from pain, but fury so sharp it carved through her vocal cords like ice. "You knew her. You used her. And when she became inconvenient...when she started to matter....you erased her."

He looked like he might vomit. "What? No. I..I didn't—"

"She was eighteen." Her voice twisted into something lethal. "She was still filling out college applications. She was a kid. And you! You turned her into a cautionary tale. A corpse."

"I didn't—what are you saying?" His voice rose in panic, hands shaking. "I never laid a hand on her, I swear!"

"You violated her," she snapped. "You watched her unravel and you did nothing. You didn't just hurt her, Alexei. You annihilated her."

"I didn't—" He stepped back, hitting the edge of the couch like he didn't know it was there. "I didn't know she was—She never said—"

"She couldn't say anything!" Love shouted. "She was terrified. She wrote about you in her journals, her drawings. She used your words like they were scripture."

His voice cracked. "I don't—I didn't think it was—" He blinked hard, like if he shut his eyes tightly enough, this would all fold into a nightmare. "I thought she was just... she was just a kid, I didn't think she—God."

"You didn't think," she echoed coldly. "That's the one thing you're good at."

"I tried to help her," he said, barely audible, voice hoarse from trying to breathe through his panic. "I did—I swear I did—"

"Then why didn't you tell me?" she spat. "Why pretend like she was nothing? Why sit there every time I said her name and act like you'd never even heard it before?"

He opened his mouth. Nothing came.

"You built a future with me on the ashes of her life," she said, voice low, tremoring with something deeper than rage. "You loved me on her grave."

Alexei's legs finally gave out. He slid down the couch until he was on the floor, hunched, face in his hands, shoulders shaking. "I didn't want this," he muttered. "I told her it would end badly—"

"She was alone," Love whispered, her throat burning. "And afraid. And pregnant."

His head jerked up. "What? No...I told her to stop...."

Told her to stop?!" she screamed, the words cracking like a snapped bone. "She was pregnant, and you let her bleed out alone, like she was nothing."

"That's not—" he gasped. "I didn't—Love, no. That's not me."

"Oh, but this is the part that was you," she said.

She let the silence stretch—taut, trembling.

"I was pregnant too."

His breath caught, eyes darting to hers like a man who'd just been told he was already dead.

"Was?" he whispered.

"I carried you inside me," she said, voice as dead as winter. "You grew in me like a weed. Like rot. I couldn't sleep without tasting iron in my mouth. I couldn't eat without hearing her scream. And every time I felt it move, it was like her ghost was inside me, kicking at the walls."

"Stop—" he whispered. "Please stop."

"I went to the clinic alone. You know what I told them?" She smiled, and it was the kind of smile that made the air turn cold. "That I wanted it out. Like it was a tumor. I didn't cry. I didn't hesitate. I watched them tear it out of me and I felt relieved."

He curled in on himself like the pain was physical now. "Why would you—why would you do that?"

"Because it was yours," she hissed. "Because every cell it grew was dipped in your lies. Because I'd rather scrape my uterus clean with a rusty knife than bring another version of you into the world. I couldn't keep your filth inside of me."

He sobbed, full-bodied and wrecked. "You didn't have to do that. I would've—I could've—"

"You?" she laughed, sharp and joyless. "You would've what? Cradled it like a redemption arc? Taught it how to lie with your eyes?"

His mouth moved, but the words were tangled. "I didn't want this. I didn't want any of this."

She reached into her hoodie.

He froze.

The metal gleamed under the dim light like it had been waiting to come home.

He didn't run.

He didn't plead.

He just looked at her like she was the last star in a dying universe.

"Choose your last words," Love hissed. "Make them count."

"I loved you..." he whispered.

"And I loved you," she said, raising the gun. Her hands were steady. Her heart was not. "'But here, on this blood-soaked field, love is a death sentence."

"I'm sorry," he breathed. "God, Love, please."

"I loved you," she said again. "And that's what I'll never forgive."

He reached for her—not physically, just a final, desperate lunge of soul toward soul. "This isn't you..."

She shook her head, slowly.

"No," she said. "It's all that's left of me."

And softer:

"You should've told me."

The shot echoed through the apartment like a curse.

Alexei's body jerked once, then crumpled like paper soaked in blood. He hit the floor with a dull, final sound—no gasp, no last words. Just an end.

Blood soaked into the floorboards, warm and dark and steady.

She didn't cry.

She stood there, smoke rising from the barrel, chest rising and falling like she was still waiting for her own name to be called.

Then her knees gave out.

She didn't collapse into sorrow. She folded into silence. Her gun clattered beside her.

Alexei's eyes were still open. Staring at nothing. Or maybe still trying to see her.

She crawled toward him, not to help, not to grieve, but to see. To truly see the thing she had once loved, the fragile myth she had crafted inside herself and named Alexei. He was no longer beautiful. He was no longer terrifying. He was only flesh now, slipping away from the story she had written for him.

The silence pressed around her, heavier than grief itself. It thickened the air, making each breath feel like drowning. It was the kind of stillness that comes only after a scream has torn through years and finally collapsed into nothing.

Her hand drifted to the blood pooling across the floor. She pressed her palm into it, feeling the heat radiating into her skin. It was warm. It was real. It clung to her fingers, her lifeline to a reality she could no longer escape.

No amount of water would ever wash it away.

Chapter 30:

Tiny Fractures

T he gunshot didn't end the silence, it created a new one. A silence so dense it filled the apartment like smoke, curling into corners, settling between the furniture, coiling around her limbs. It hung in the air, thick and breathless, the kind of silence that doesn't wait for an answer because it is the answer. One moment ago, this space was still pretending to be a home, a haven built on lies. Now it was nothing more than a tomb.

Love didn't move. Her hand remained outstretched, fingers locked around the gun, as if her body hadn't yet received the message that it was done. That the final word had been spoken, that the story had ended with a single echo and the absence that followed. A thread of smoke drifted upward from the barrel, delicate and slow, spiraling like a ghost released from its shell. And across the room, Alexei had slumped to the floor beneath the windows, his body folded awkwardly, blood blooming beneath him in a dark, quiet pool that stretched toward her like a reaching shadow.

She didn't flinch. Couldn't. Her lungs forgot their purpose, and her legs—once so sure, so strong—had turned to stone. The only thing still alive inside her was the relentless pulse in her ears, a pounding, deafening rhythm that seemed to mock the stillness all around her. She stared not at the blood, not at the weapon in her hand, but at his face. That face she had memorized in the dark. The curve of his mouth. The line of his lashes. The eyes that always held too much.

That look. That final look before she pulled the trigger had not been fear. It had not been anger. It had not even been guilt.

It had been heartbreak.

Something inside her fractured, not loudly, not with any grand collapse. Just a hairline crack, so fine it was almost invisible, but permanent all the same. A fracture in the version of herself she thought she understood.

There was no movement from him. No flicker of breath, no twitch of a limb. He did not reach for her. He did not gasp. He did not beg her to take it back.

She waited for something, anything—a sign that she had been right, that this had been justice, that this had been righteous, but there was nothing. Only the terrible, suffocating stillness of a world that refused to tell her she had been right at all.

The doubt began to bloom slowly, rising from the splintered ruins inside her chest, creeping through her like mold spreading through walls left too long in the dark.

Her body jolted, as if ripped awake from a dream, and she stumbled backward. Her heel caught the edge of the rug and sent her crashing to her knees, her palms slapping against the hardwood with a dull, broken sound. The gun slipped from her fingers and skidded across the floor, coming to a stop beneath the coffee table.

She stared at it, breathless, dazed. It looked like it had always been there. Like it had been waiting all along, biding its time until it became part of the story she could never undo.

The breath finally came. And with it, the shaking.

She crawled backward, away from the body, unable to take her eyes off the spot where he'd fallen. Her stomach twisted in on itself, bile rising to the back of her throat. She turned, crawling toward the keypad with hands that didn't feel like hers, fingers fumbling, vision swimming. She missed the code once. Then again. Her whole body shook. Her head throbbed. Her body was present, but her mind had already fractured into a hundred pieces.

The door unlocked with a soft, traitorous click.

She ran.

Down the hall, across the lobby, into the night. The air hit her face like a slap—cold and damp, thick with the smell of rain and asphalt. She kept running until the sound of her shoes against the pavement drowned out the sound of her thoughts. Her legs didn't know where they were going. They simply moved forward, carrying her like a marionette with its strings frayed.

She reached her car several blocks away, fumbling for her keys with trembling hands. She dropped them once. Twice. Got the door open on the third try and collapsed into the driver's seat, her breath catching against the sob clawing its way out of her chest. She turned the ignition with a hand that barely obeyed her. The engine growled to life. She pulled onto the street, eyes wide and wild, the city blurring around her in streaks of wet light and motion.

She drove with no destination, no sense of direction, only the instinct to move. To get away from the red, the silence, the unbearable image of his body crumpled beneath her window. But she couldn't drive away from what was already inside her. It was too late for that. The guilt wasn't on her hands. It was under her skin.

His voice echoed in her ears. His laugh. His touch. That gentle way he used to press his lips to the center of her forehead when she said she couldn't sleep. The way he whispered lyubov moya like it meant something holy.

The look on his face before she ended it.

The silence. The stillness.

The way he didn't try to save himself.

She pulled into the empty lot by the harbor and slammed the brakes, flinging the door open just in time to collapse onto the pavement and retch. There was nothing inside her to bring up—no food, no drink—just bile and grief and all the pieces of herself that had shattered when he didn't fight back.

She pressed her forehead to the cold concrete, breath heaving, tears flooding the spaces behind her eyes but refusing to fall. Her body convulsed once, twice, before she forced herself upright and crawled back into the car. She grabbed her phone and dialed with fingers that barely cooperated.

James answered on the third ring.

"James," she gasped, her voice breaking, falling apart in real time. "James—I did it. I—I shot him. He's gone—I think he's really gone—I don't know what to—"

There was silence on the other end. Not shock. Not disbelief.

Just silence.

Then: "Okay. Listen to me. You need to calm down."

Her breath caught in her throat.

He wasn't surprised.

"I—he said things, James! He mentioned Ophelia. He looked scared, I don't know if he was lying, I don't know—"

"Love," James interrupted, his voice too measured, too smooth. "Did anyone see you leave?"

She blinked. "What? I—I don't think so—I didn't—why are you—what the hell is going on?"

"Wipe the call log when we hang up. Drive back to the apartment like you're just arriving...Make sure someone sees you so they can be a witness to you coming in. Take the long route. Don't speak to anyone. Not Layla. Not your parents. I'll take care of the rest."

Love went still.

The cold inside her deepened.

"You'll... what?"

"I'll make the call. Break-in. Wrong place. Wrong time. It'll be clean. Just do exactly as I say."

The line went dead.

She stared down at her phone, still glowing faintly in her lap, her heart frozen mid-beat.

No questions.

No what happened?

No are you okay?

No why did you do it?

He was ready. Too ready.

And something in her—something deeper than her breath, deeper than her guilt—realized what that meant.

He wasn't shocked.

He wasn't horrified.

He had a plan.

She closed her eyes, let the cold consume her.

Because now, it wasn't just Alexei's blood on her hands.

It was the possibility that he had told the truth.

And if that was true—if she had pulled the trigger on a man who was innocent—then what came next wasn't grief.

It was damnation.

The first cracks had formed.

Tiny fractures in her logic.

In her certainty.

In her sense of self.

And somewhere deep inside, beneath the roar of her pulse and the silence left behind by his death, a single truth whispered its way through the fog:

Why doesn't this feel like justice?

Chapter 31

Cry On Demand

The blood hadn't dried yet. It was still clinging to the seams of the wood floor, glistening in places where the light hit too directly. James had worked fast. Love had driven away just as he told her to—shaky hands on the wheel, headlights slicing through the dark like she hadn't just left a corpse cooling on the rug. She parked two blocks down. Waited. Counted the seconds. Then returned, pulling up like she was just now discovering the nightmare.

It had to look like she hadn't been there. That she had stumbled in on something violent, not created it. James had wiped what he could. Scrubbed what wouldn't stain deeper. He said he'd handle the cameras. She didn't ask how. All she knew was that by the time she walked back through that door, he'd already made it look like someone else had been here.

Her shoes were back on now. Her sweater was zipped halfway up. Her hair was damp from the sink. The bathroom smelled like soap and adrenaline.

"Sit on the couch," James said, not unkindly. His voice was steady, measured, not too loud. "They'll be here in less than five minutes. You need to be crying. Not calm."

"I can't cry on command," she whispered.

"Then shake. Breathe loud. You're scared. You're pregnant. You came home and found him like this. That's all."

Love didn't move. The couch felt too far away. Her legs too thin beneath her. But she stumbled into the frame of the room and lowered herself, trying not to look at the body. The rug covered most of it now. There was no outline, no pool, just the stain that would never fully leave the fibers.

The knock was sharp. Three times. Official.

James didn't answer immediately. He wiped his hands once more on a towel and walked to the door like he wasn't covered in invisible guilt.

Love started to tremble. A practiced kind of trembling, the way she used to fake being sick in high school—just enough fever in the eyes to sell it. She wrapped her arms around her belly. Her breath hitched. She counted to three. Then five. Then she let out a sound that was somewhere between a sob and a gasp.

James opened the door.

"Sir, we received a call about a possible break-in. You made the report?"

"Yes," James said. "I'm her friend. She called me before she called anyone else. I got here as fast as I could. I—I think she's in shock."

Love looked up, blinking rapidly, as if just now noticing the officers.

"Oh my god," she whispered, curling into herself. "Oh my god, he's—he's dead, isn't he? Please, please—"

"Ma'am, I need you to stay calm," one of the officers said, already stepping into the room. The other was radioing for backup, forensics, someone to start cataloging the mess James had carefully manufactured.

"I came home and the door was open, I didn't know—I didn't think—" Love's voice cracked. "I just wanted to tell him, I wanted to say we—we were going to tell the family tonight."

"Tell them what?" the officer asked gently.

Love pressed a hand to her stomach.

"Oh," he said, and the tone shifted. "I understand. I'm very sorry. Can you walk me through what happened?"

She looked at James, then looked away, blinking hard.

"I went to school and then to my internship as I usually do," she murmured. "I came back and the lights were off. The lock looked fine, but the door wasn't latched. I stepped inside and I saw—"

She let the sentence drop.

"We'll need to take your statement. And his," the officer nodded to James.

James nodded. "Of course."

Love let them walk past. She didn't have to look to know they'd find nothing out of place. No signs of forced entry. Just disarray. Just enough struggle to raise the right questions, and just enough confusion to make those questions turn into theories instead of accusations.

James sat beside her as the officers began their examination. One moved toward Alexei's body, now partially covered by the throw from the couch, and pulled on gloves with practiced precision. The other walked the perimeter of the room, jotting down notes, pointing out scuff marks, asking for a flashlight. When the coroner arrived minutes later, they didn't say much—just exchanged clipped words and set up quietly, unfolding a stretcher near the doorway.

Love shrank into herself at the sound of the zipper. She could barely keep her eyes on them as they cataloged every piece of the scene, as gloved hands reached under Alexei's neck, lifting and shifting him to the body bag.

"Do you know if anything's missing?" one of the officers asked James, glancing toward the bookshelf.

"The drawer over there," James replied, voice carefully weighted. "Looks like it was rummaged. His watch isn't on the nightstand. His laptop's still here though. Might've been interrupted."

The officer scribbled something down. "We'll dust for prints. Someone might've worn gloves, but it's still worth running."

Love pressed her hand to her stomach and turned her face into the crook of her arm. She didn't want to see the stretcher move. She didn't want to hear the velcro hiss closed.

"She shouldn't be here for this part," one officer said under his breath.

"She didn't want to leave," James murmured. "And she's not alone."

"You okay?" he whispered.

"No," she whispered back.

"You're doing great."

She wanted to scream.

The night blurred after that. Statements were taken. Her voice trembled in the right places. James put a hand on her shoulder once. She didn't flinch, but she noticed how steady his pulse felt under his thumb.

She kept waiting for him to crack. To stumble. To slip up. But he never did. Not once.

When the officers left them alone again, James handed her a glass of water.

"You should lie down soon. You're not going to get much sleep, but your body will shut down if you don't at least try."

She took the glass. She drank.

"You're not shaken," she said finally.

James looked at her. "What?"

"You're calm. You were calm the whole time."

His mouth moved once, then settled into a line.

"Someone had to be."

She stared at him, eyes slightly narrowed.

"I'm not judging you," she said.

"I didn't think you were."

But she was thinking. Thinking too much. About the way he'd known exactly what to say. About the way he'd moved through the apartment like he had practiced. Like he'd always known this might happen.

"You don't have to trust me," James said, as if he'd read her thoughts. "But I'm on your side."

Love didn't answer.

She was too tired. Too frayed. Too cold.

"Let's get through the night first," she said.

James nodded.

And the silence that settled between them was not comfortable.

It was something else entirely.

Something that neither of them dared name just yet.

Chapter 32:

S ***ergei Chervyakov***
    The sky was too blue.
    That was the first thing Love noticed as she stepped out of the car. A brilliant, cutting kind of blue—mocking in its beauty, too serene for the day they were burying a man she once loved. A man she had killed.

The funeral was held in a private chapel far from the city's din, nestled between sculpted hedges and stone angels that lined the walk like silent sentries. Everything about the place whispered wealth: the polished stone beneath her heels, the stark, smooth silence, the scent of lilies too carefully arranged to feel like grief. Even the mourners moved like they'd practiced, like they'd rehearsed how to cry without smudging anything.

It felt sterile. Curated. Sanitized mourning, airbrushed tragedy.

Love walked toward the entrance, black fabric swaying with every step. Her dress was flawless—tailored to trace the soft curve of her stomach, the quiet implication of a child that would never exist. Her heels sank into the damp grass as she passed through the chapel doors. Her face, painted with pale foundation and subtly smudged liner, looked perfectly undone, like someone had tried to cover up days of crying and almost succeeded.

She hadn't slept. She hadn't eaten. But she didn't look broken.

She looked believable.

The chapel was small and cold, the kind of sacred space designed less for comfort and more for control. The pews were arranged in tight, uncomfortable rows. White lilies framed the mahogany casket at the altar—dozens of them, pristine and sharp with scent. There were no photos. No music. No slideshow of memories. Just the dull echo of footsteps and the occasional murmur of someone trying not to speak too loudly.

Alexei would've hated it.

She moved to the front row and sat alone, folding her hands just beneath her stomach. A thousand eyes lingered on her without landing. The tragic girlfriend. The widow-to-be. So brave. So young. So pregnant. They pitied her, which was exactly what she needed them to do.

She stared at the casket like she was trying to bore through it with her eyes.

There was no peace in her chest. No triumph. Just a low, constant hum—like she was vibrating under her skin, like her blood had turned to static. She had expected resolution. She had expected something cleaner. But all she felt was tension. Like a scream that had been swallowed and couldn't find its way back up.

She imagined his body inside the box. Still. Cold. Lifeless. And the image didn't bring closure.

It brought nausea.

A clipboard-wielding woman approached at one point, handing her tissues she didn't need. Someone behind her sniffled. Another person quietly clicked their phone screen, checking the time.

She didn't recognize half the people here. Most wore suits too polished to belong to family. Business associates. Investors. Employees. Mourning felt secondary. The entire ceremony felt more like a financial quarterly—tidy, rehearsed, quietly brutal.

The seat beside her remained empty far too long before someone finally filled it.

James slid into place, late and rumpled, his tie loosened, his eyes red but dry. He didn't speak. Didn't look at her. Just held the folded funeral program like it might crumble in his hands if he let go.

She felt something stir when she saw him—anger maybe, or resentment for how quiet he'd gone since it happened. She tugged at his shirt, looking for some comfort.

"James...you won't even look at me? I thought we were in this togeth-"

"No, Love. We aren't." he cut her off. "I'm sick of latching onto secrets."

He didn't wait for a response, and walked away as if he couldn't bear to hear anything else.

Love stood alone in her shame...but it was shortlived as she felt prying eyes on her.

A presence colder than the chapel's marble floor.

When she turned, he was already analyzing her.

Sergei Chervyakov.

Alexei's father stood at the edge of the aisle, arms folded behind his back, as if he were inspecting a failed building project. His suit was immaculate, slate-gray and severe. His silver hair was combed back with precision. And his eyes—sharp, unblinking—sliced through her like a scalpel.

They didn't shake hands. He didn't offer condolences. He simply nodded, once, like he was acknowledging a particularly unfortunate spreadsheet.

"I see," he said flatly.

Love blinked. "I... I just wanted to say I'm sorry. For your loss."

"There is no loss," he replied, his voice smooth and cold. "There is absence. Loss implies I did not plan for contingency."

She stared at him, unsure if she had heard correctly. "He was your son."

"Yes. And now he is gone." Sergei's tone didn't shift. "One must accept the consequences."

Her fingers dug into the fabric of her dress. Anger flared somewhere behind her ribs, but it didn't make it to her mouth.

Before she could respond, someone stepped between them.

Felix.

He moved with soft confidence, like he'd been waiting for his cue. A hand came to rest on her shoulder—light enough to appear protective, steady enough to assert possession.

"Sergei," he said gently, "you're scaring her."

Sergei barely turned his head. "You shouldn't be here either."

Felix smiled, all grace and polish. "I'm here to pay my respects."

"Respect," Sergei echoed, as if the word itself offended him. "You don't pay respect. You build it. With empire. With blood."

And just like that, he turned and walked away.

Love exhaled, shaky and shallow. Her chest felt scraped raw.

"Don't take him personally," Felix murmured beside her. "He doesn't believe in grief. Only in weakness."

She tried to nod, but her body didn't cooperate. Her limbs felt borrowed, disconnected.

Then, too casually, Felix added, "Didn't Alexei mention I'm his half-brother?"

Her head snapped toward him. "What?"

He blinked, caught off guard by her tone. "I thought he had."

"No," she said, sharper now, some ache rising through her. "He didn't. You're—what? Half-brother?"

Felix gave a small shrug. "Same father. Different mothers. We weren't close. Didn't grow up together."

Her mouth opened. Closed. She searched his face.

"Why didn't you say anything?"

His gaze didn't falter. "Because it wasn't relevant to our conversations. And honestly, it was Alexei's place to tell you. We didn't associate. Not really."

He said it kindly. Gently. Like he was explaining a harmless omission. But every word struck like a hammer.

Not relevant.

Love blinked hard. The sanctuary lights felt too bright now. The sound of the priest's voice in the background blurred into a dull buzz.

Her fingers pressed against her temples. Her breath caught in her throat.

Felix had known the entire time.

He'd watched her unravel. He'd seen her spiral. And never once had he mentioned that the man she thought was helping her understand Alexei was, in fact, his brother.

And now, standing beside her in front of Alexei's casket, he spoke like he was discussing the weather.

She thought of the countless times he had comforted her, the way he always seemed to appear just as her doubts began to rise. He had woven the story she needed with such ease, feeding it to her in pieces until she clung to it like the only thing that could save her.

He had not pulled the trigger. He had only placed the gun in her hands and turned away while she learned how to use it.

Her legs gave out beneath her, and she dropped into the pew, the air tearing from her lungs in broken gasps. She gripped the edge of the bench, as if holding on could keep her from sliding deeper into the void that was already swallowing her whole.

Felix followed, concern painted neatly across his face. "Are you alright?"

"I'm fine," she said, the words scraped raw from her throat.

"It's a lot," he murmured. "I'm sorry. I shouldn't have brought it up now. Families are complicated. The Chervyakovs, doubly so."

Love didn't respond. Her nails pressed crescent moons into her palms. She stared at the floor as if it would offer her answers.

She had loved Alexei with rage, with fear, with the kind of desperation that carved its name into every hollow part of her. She had loved him until there was nothing left to love, and then she had killed him.

No sob escaped her, no cry broke through the ruin inside her chest. Only a single tear slipped free, cold against her skin as it traced the curve of her cheek and fell, landing on the stone floor with a sound too soft to be real, yet somehow louder than everything else in the room.

She did not know if it was a tear for Alexei, or for the girl she had once been, before she ever crossed paths with his brother and learned what it meant to lose everything she thought she knew.

Chapter 33:

C *ircling Satellites*

     The days after the funeral moved like static beneath her skin—too bright, too quiet, too clean. The world continued its motion, but for Love, everything had stilled. Life no longer moved in time. It hovered, paused mid-step, as if she had been sealed inside amber. Conversations passed by muffled, meals came and went unnoticed, and light fell through windows at unnatural angles. Everything around her looked real. But none of it felt alive.

Her grief had become a performance. And she was still stuck in costume.

She'd stayed at Alexei's apartment for days after his death, draped in the illusion of cherishing his memory—folding his clothes with trembling hands, running her fingers over the spine of his books, lighting a candle near his desk she never really intended to watch burn. To the outside world, she was the grieving partner lost in nostalgia. But that apartment wasn't sacred. It was a tomb with carpeted floors and untouched mail, and the longer she stayed there, the more it smelled like blood beneath lemon-scented cleaner. So when her parents pressed harder—when their concerned visits became more frequent, when Dahlia began bringing bags of soup she would never eat and Ashton started asking pointed, silent questions—she finally gave in.

She told them the grief was too much. That she wanted to be surrounded by love. That she didn't want to be alone.

It wasn't true, but it was convenient.

So, she moved back home.

Her bedroom was clean, scented with lavender, and the bed was perfectly made. Her desk sat untouched beneath old stationery. Ophelia's door stayed closed at the end of the hallway like it had teeth behind it.

Her parents hovered without quite colliding—Dahlia flitting around the house like a moth that had forgotten what flame meant, and Ashton drifting like smoke. He didn't speak unless necessary. And when he did, it always sounded like something else waited beneath the words.

Dahlia came into her room most often, always with something in her hands—a bowl, a folded shirt, a question she didn't want to voice. She kept her tone light, but her eyes searched constantly, as if expecting Love to crack open mid-sentence. One afternoon, while folding laundry that didn't need folding, Dahlia paused mid-sleeve.

"You've lost weight," she murmured, tone too even. "Is the baby okay?"

Love didn't flinch. "Yes, Mom. Everything's fine."

The lie passed easily. Too easily. It didn't even taste bitter anymore.

Ashton was less delicate. He watched her like a man who knew something wasn't right and couldn't yet prove it. One evening, she stepped out of the shower to find him standing just outside the bathroom door, arms crossed, face unreadable.

"You haven't said much," he said.

"There's not much to say."

He nodded, slow. "Hiding things doesn't make them go away. Especially when people start asking questions."

She didn't respond. Didn't blink. Just moved past him, water still clinging to her skin, her towel wrapped too tightly. He didn't follow. Just let the words hang in the air like smoke from a match no one bothered to blow out.

She started avoiding mirrors. The hallway one was covered with a towel, the bathroom one fogged over every time she showered, and she let it stay that way. She didn't recognize herself in reflections anymore. The copper of her hair dulled to rust. Her cheeks hollowed, shadows blooming beneath her eyes like bruises that had forgotten how they got there. The only part of her face that still felt real were her eyes—and they belonged to someone haunted. Someone hunted.

At night, she dreamed of him.

Not always dead. Not always bleeding. Sometimes he was simply standing there, on the far side of the room, watching her with that same quiet patience he'd always had. Sometimes he reached for her, his fingers ghosting through the air. Sometimes he said her name like it was a promise. But he never came closer. And he never smiled.

She stopped sleeping in her bed. Curled up on the floor instead, wrapped in blankets like armor. The mattress felt like a mouth that wanted to swallow her whole.

The first time Felix showed up after the funeral, it was just after sunset. The sky was still bruised with remnants of gold, and Love had been sitting alone in the kitchen, turning a tea bag in cold water out of habit more than thirst. She didn't hear him arrive. Only saw his reflection in the glass of the back door.

She startled, standing abruptly. "Why are you here?"

He held up a paper bag like it was some kind of peace offering. "Just thought you might need a few things. Soup. Crackers. Some protein shakes."

"I didn't ask you to come."

"I know," he said, voice steady, unbothered. "But I figured it didn't matter."

She stared at him, eyes narrowing, arms crossed so tightly across her chest it almost hurt. "You could've texted."

"You wouldn't have answered."

He was right. And that made it worse.

He stepped inside like he'd been invited, moved quietly, efficiently—setting things down on the counter, peeling the labels off the cans before placing them in the cupboard. Like this was some unspoken ritual. Like he had done this before.

"I don't need help," she muttered.

"I'm not here to help. Just... to be nearby. In case."

"In case of what?"

He didn't answer. Just glanced at her once, eyes unreadable, and then moved to the sink to rinse his hands as if they were dirtied by grief and not implication.

She didn't know how to be around him.

Maybe because he was calm when she wasn't.

Maybe because silence had started to feel heavier than company.

Or maybe... because part of her was waiting to see what he'd do next.

He stuck around like grief's shadow, like something dark that lingered where the light just missed. He didn't knock. Just showed up. Left flowers on the kitchen counter. Grief counseling pamphlets folded too neatly. Groceries with the labels peeled off, as if names were too loud, too vulgar for mourning. He never overstayed. He never made demands. He always spoke softly, like a nurse approaching a skittish patient.

She didn't ask him to stop. It was easier than asking him to leave.

"You've barely been eating," he said once, placing a silent meal on the stove. "I remember that look. Like your body forgot how to want things."

She didn't respond. She sat on the couch with her knees to her chest, eyes trained on the window that refused to fog no matter how close she breathed.

Felix didn't press. He never did. He lingered, hovered—always just close enough to be useful, never close enough to be touched. And yet, the more she watched him move around the house, the more it unnerved her. The way he handled her grief like it was something familiar. Predictable. As if he'd already calculated the half-life of her mourning and was just biding his time until it decayed into silence.

She thought back to the funeral, the way he'd said it so easily: Didn't Alexei mention I'm his half-brother?

Like it was trivia.

Like it was nothing.

She hadn't known. And when she'd looked at him, really looked, his expression hadn't shifted. No remorse. No awkwardness. Just that same calm detachment, like he was observing her heartbreak, not participating in it. He never brought it up again. And neither did she.

But the memory lodged itself in her throat like a bone she couldn't swallow. Every time he stepped closer, every time his hand hovered near hers or his voice gentled at the edges, something inside her screamed—not because of what he said.

But because of what he refused to.

That night, when the ceiling above her bed became too much to look at, she slipped from her room and wandered down the hall. Ophelia's door opened without protest. The air inside was still. She sat on the edge of her sister's bed and stared at the desk for a long while before opening the old laptop tucked beneath the dresser. Then, on impulse, she grabbed the password they used for everything, her sister's birthday, and opened Ophelia's email.

The inbox was full of the mundane. Sale notifications, writing contests, scholarship rejections, college prep reminders. It looked like someone who had plans. Someone who had believed there'd be more time.

She almost closed the browser, but then she saw it—one message, flagged, buried deep.

To: F.S.

Her breath stalled. The name on the email chilled her.

The body of the message was brief. Polite. Harmless.

Just wanted to thank you again for your time last week. The feedback really helped.

Hope the portfolio looks better now. You've been so kind.

—O.

Love stared at the screen for a long time, chest hollowing like something had just been scooped out of it with both hands. Her fingers hovered over the keyboard. She didn't need to guess who F.S. was. She already knew.

A memory surfaced—Ophelia curled beside her in bed one night, eyes bright, voice bubbling over.

"I think he really believes in me. He listens. Like... really listens."

Love had muttered something distractedly, barely looking up from her textbook. She never asked who he was.

Now she wished she had.

She closed the laptop slowly, almost tenderly, as if disturbing it might somehow undo what she had seen, might call something back that had already been lost.

Tears came then, silent and bitter, not because she missed Ophelia, but because she realized she had never truly known her. Not in the ways that mattered. Not in the ways that could have saved her.

Someone else had known her. Someone else had seen the parts she had never touched.

In her blind grief, Love had destroyed the only man who might have loved her with his whole heart, sacrificing him for a girl who had never asked to be saved. In doing so, she had taken the last sacred thing she carried within herself, the last piece that was still clean, and offered it up to the fire, calling it his filth to make the burning easier to endure.

Now there was nothing left inside her to cleanse. Only ashes, and the weight of all she had chosen not to see.

Chapter 34:

S it Up, Ophelia. Now.

The house wasn't quiet in a peaceful way. It was the kind of silence that clung to the walls after something had died inside them—thick, unmoving, ashen. It didn't settle gently; it pressed down, filled the rooms like a second ceiling. The air didn't feel breathable. It felt like grief made visible. Even the sunlight was wrong. It filtered through the blinds like it didn't belong there, as if the house had rejected brightness entirely.

Love had been home for weeks, though the word no longer meant anything. She moved through the house like a ghost that hadn't realized it was dead. She ate when Dahlia placed food in front of her. She responded when Ashton offered conversation in careful, clipped sentences. She slept when her body collapsed, not when she found rest. Her spirit stayed curled somewhere behind her ribs, too tired to resurface. She had done what she came to do. She had punished the man who ruined her sister. She had pulled the trigger. She had paid for blood with blood. But the ache inside her had not lessened. It had simply lost its urgency.

Felix had not gone anywhere.

He kept coming like clockwork, as if his presence were medicinal. He knocked with the same rhythm. He spoke with the same gentle tone. He offered herbal teas, folded blankets, printed poems, and vitamin bottles wrapped in soft paper towels. He never asked for anything. He never imposed. But his timing was always precise. He left before the silence got too heavy. He knew when to linger and when to disappear. He always managed to say the right thing—phrases that sounded tender if you didn't look too closely. Things like,

"Grief is just love with nowhere to go." Things like, "Healing takes time, and so do answers."

Once, those lines had soothed her. Now, they made her stomach turn.

She used to think his presence was comfort. Lately, it had started to feel like surveillance dressed as compassion. And tonight, something finally shifted.

She found herself once again outside Ophelia's bedroom door, standing in the exact place where everything had begun to fall apart. The last time she stepped through that doorway, she had found a sentence hidden in her sister's notebook. A sentence that echoed with such specificity, such intimacy, that it collapsed her entire world. Catching moonlight in a jar. Alexei had said it aloud days earlier, casually, like it belonged to him. But it didn't. It belonged to Ophelia. And Love had interpreted that one sentence as proof—proof that Alexei had lied, had known her sister, had betrayed them both. It was the phrase that led to the bullet. It was the moment she stopped asking questions and started planning his death.

And now, she was here again. But this time, she wasn't looking for clarity.

She was looking for whatever still refused to leave her alone.

The door creaked open. Dust met her in the air, dancing through the light like particles of memory. The lavender scent of Ophelia's shampoo clung to the room like a secret that hadn't yet faded. Everything was still in place—the scarf hanging off the back of the desk chair, the chipped lamp, the stack of sketchbooks leaning precariously to one side. Nothing had changed since she last came in here. But Love had. Her mind was no longer certain of what she had done. Her heart no longer knew what had been real.

She sat at the edge of the bed, her hands resting in her lap. Her fingers were curled, her nails faintly digging into the skin of her palm. For a long time, she just stared at the floorboards. Her voice, when it finally came, felt unfamiliar.

"I did it."

It wasn't a question. It wasn't a confession. It was a fact, spoken aloud to the silence in case it had forgotten.

"I made him bleed for you. I made him pay. I looked him in the eye and believed I was delivering justice."

She turned her head, letting her gaze fall toward the desk.

"So why doesn't it feel like you came back to me?"

She stood and crossed the room. Her hands moved over the surface of the desk like she was retracing old wounds. The last time she had opened drawers and flipped through her sister's things, it had been out of anger. She had been seeking confirmation, not truth. She had wanted to find enough to make herself feel right.

Tonight, she wasn't trying to be right. She just couldn't carry the questions anymore.

She bent down to sift through the notebooks. Her fingers brushed over pages filled with half-drawn portraits, lines of poetry that trailed into empty space, and margins scribbled with anxious thoughts too disorganized to make sense. And then she found it.

The laptop.

She remembered picking it up once before. She had held it, thought about opening it, and then placed it back down like it was a weapon she wasn't ready to use. But now she had already destroyed everything. What more could this hold?

She plugged it in. The screen blinked to life. There was no password. The desktop bloomed in clutter. Screenshots, folders, open essays, abandoned messages. Then she saw it—a folder tucked in the corner. Titled in lowercase, plain and possessive: mine.

She opened it.

Inside, there were two video files. Neither had names. Neither had thumbnails.

Something in her gut tightened as she clicked the first one.

The screen flickered. The video quality was poor, grainy and disjointed. The camera was resting on what looked like a side table or the floor. A lamp in the corner buzzed, giving the whole room a sickly glow. Then Ophelia came into frame.

Love's breath left her lungs like something physical had been pulled out of her.

Her sister didn't look fragile. She looked obliterated. Her face was pale and bruised, the skin around her eyes swollen and her lips raw and split open. Her hair was unwashed, her posture hunched as though even sitting up had become an unbearable task. Dried blood ringed her nostrils. Her cheek was marked with what looked like the shape of fingers. Her mouth trembled when she spoke, the words forcing themselves out like they were being rehearsed.

"I love him," she said, and the smile that followed was so wrong it made Love's stomach twist. "He says we're going to get married."

Her gaze shifted offscreen, and for a moment, she flinched. Her shoulders tightened.

"He says I ruin things when I talk too much. That I should be quiet. That I ask stupid questions."

The room behind her was still. Too still. Ophelia's voice dropped to a whisper.

"I told him I'd stay. I told him I wouldn't tell anyone. He says I'm finally starting to understand him."

She leaned closer to the camera and forced one last line.

"Baby... are we gonna get married?"

The screen went black.

The second video began automatically.

Ophelia was curled on the floor now, her knees drawn to her chest, her hair hiding her face. Her arms were wrapped around her legs. Her shirt was stained. Her mouth looked freshly bloodied, her bottom lip swollen and cut. Her eye was puffy, nearly shut. She rocked slowly and mumbled the same words over and over.

"I said I was sorry. I wasn't supposed to cry. I ruin everything when I cry. I said I was sorry."

A shadow moved just beyond the frame. A figure, shifting closer.

Then a voice spoke—flat, cold, and commanding.

"Sit up, Ophelia. Now."

Love knew the voice.

"Sit up! Now. You know better."

She knew it the way she knew her own name.

It was Felix.

It wasn't a hallucination or a memory misfiring. It was his voice, untouched by distortion, clear and real. He had been in that room. He had done this. He had controlled her sister until she disappeared inside herself.

And then he had walked into Love's life and called himself her friend.

She slammed the laptop shut with a force that rattled the desk. Her breath vanished. Her vision blurred. Her body surged to its feet. She ran.

She didn't know what she was doing until she was already moving—out of the room, down the hallway, through the front door. The air outside struck her face like a wave. She barely made it onto the lawn before her body convulsed. She doubled over and vomited, violently, until there was nothing left in her but bile and brokenness. Her hands clutched at the grass. Her legs gave out beneath her.

She dropped to her knees, still shaking, mouth open, gasping for air she couldn't hold.

And then, without warning, she screamed.

The sound tore up from her chest like it had been buried there for years.

"HOW MUCH MORE CAN A PERSON TAKE?"

The words split her open. She screamed again, and again, until her throat burned and her body collapsed forward. Her forehead pressed to the dirt, her fists clenched. The sky above No one offered her comfort. The earth beneath her stayed silent, indifferent to the ruin collapsing inside her.

Felix had stolen her sister first, stripping away something sacred before she even knew it was gone. He had unraveled her trust next, thread by thread, until nothing remained to hold her steady. Finally, he had placed the weight of a gun in her hands and watched as she destroyed the only man who might have saved her.

Now there was nothing left to protect. No illusions. No pieces to gather.

She had only the scream, ripping through her with such violence that it left her trembling and hollow. When it finally broke apart in her throat, when the tears spilled without shame, she knelt in the wreckage of herself and knew what had risen from it.

This was not guilt. It was not grief.

It was war.

Felix had crowned her its author with his own hands.

○ ○ ○ ○ ○ ○ ○ ○ ○

Chapter 35:

All the Things He Didn't Say

The morning arrived without permission. It didn't feel like a beginning, just the continuation of something that hadn't stopped burning. The sky had already turned a bruised, pale blue by the time Love sat up, though she didn't remember lying down. Her body ached in strange places, her spine heavy, her eyes swollen. It wasn't sleep she had gotten—it was collapse.

Everything around her felt too loud in the wrong way. The clink of mugs in the kitchen, the soft shuffle of Dahlia moving across the tile, Ashton's breath behind his newspaper—each sound pressed into her skin like a bruise. It was all too familiar, too rehearsed. Life continuing with the illusion of normalcy while she sat there, splintering under the weight of what she knew. Her hands rested on the edge of the kitchen table, knuckles pale from how tightly she gripped the wood. She didn't trust her own strength, not right now. Not when something inside her felt like it was shifting out of place.

Ophelia's voice still haunted the space behind her eyes. That broken whisper. That forced smile. The delicate way she'd tried to pretend it was love when it was fear draped in promises. And then the voice that followed. Smooth. Measured. Not angry. Not threatening. But absolute.

"Sit up, Ophelia. Now."

She had played it again last night. More than once. Each time, she thought she might hear it differently. That maybe she had imagined the cadence, the familiarity, the horrifying steadiness. But no matter how many times she looped it, it was him. It was Felix.

And the terrifying part wasn't just that he had done it. It was that he had watched her mourn. Sat beside her while she cried. Wiped her hands clean after she put a bullet into someone who didn't deserve it.

She sat now, unmoving, as her mother set tea in front of her. She didn't reach for it. Didn't speak. Her father's paper rustled faintly. None of it mattered. Her gaze rested on the grain of the table beneath her fingers, following the lines like they might offer a map out of this nightmare.

Felix would arrive soon. She didn't need a reminder. His visits had become clockwork. Eleven o'clock, give or take a few minutes depending on whether he wanted to appear spontaneous or considerate. He always came bearing softness—something edible, something said with quiet wisdom, something that mimicked care well enough to be mistaken for it.

But now that she had seen behind the curtain, every part of his presence felt like performance.

She didn't know how she'd missed it before. The way he lingered in doorways without making a sound. The way his concern never quite made it into his eyes. The way he always said the right thing—not because he understood, but because he studied the timing. She had welcomed him in, again and again, like a guest she didn't realize had already made himself at home.

She hated that part the most. That she had trusted him.

Still, when he knocked, she didn't stop him from entering.

He stepped into the kitchen like he always did, no hesitation. A paper bag in one hand. A subtle smile playing on his face. Not too happy, not too grim. Just the right amount of solemnity for someone who had arrived to support the grieving.

"Rye bread again," he said as he set the bag down on the counter. "Still warm. Found a place that doesn't put sugar in it. Apparently, that's rare now."

Love turned her head slowly, watching him like she was seeing through water. "You remember things like that?"

He smiled, brushing a bit of flour from the edge of the bag. "Sure. Some people remember birthdays. I remember bread."

He said it like a joke, like something charming and eccentric. Like he was harmless.

She didn't return the smile. She didn't offer any expression at all. Just silence, deep and deliberate, as she watched him begin to unpack the rest of what he brought. Two apples. A tin of soup. A clean white box of tea. Then something else—something small.

A book.

Not just any book. A poetry collection.

The title struck her first. Then the cover. Then the memory.

James had quoted from that exact collection once, months ago, while they were walking outside the Channel 5 building. Some forgettable line about stars and longing. At the time, she thought nothing of it. James had always been like that—bookish when it suited him, vulnerable only in abstract. But now, seeing it in Felix's bag, something in her chest twisted sharply.

It wasn't a new book. The spine was worn, the corners curled. The cover had a faint stain, like it had seen weather and been passed between hands.

She didn't breathe for a moment. The connection flickered across her mind like lightning. Not proof. But too coincidental to be innocent.

"Where'd you get that?" she asked, nodding slightly toward the book.

Felix glanced down, his expression unchanged. "James gave it to me," he said easily. "Said it was my kind of thing. He's always throwing books at people. Thoughtful, in a chaotic sort of way."

He smiled again, faint, nonchalant. The kind of smile that had worked on her before. But now she saw it for what it was—a shield.

Love stared at the book. That one detail should have meant nothing. But now it felt like a thread pulled loose from everything. Not just the poetry. Not just the timing. But the fact that Felix hadn't even blinked when she asked. Like he already had the answer ready.

That night, long after the house had gone still and the air had returned to its stiff silence, Love sat alone in her room, the laptop warm against her legs. Her screen glowed faintly, an empty document waiting for her to give it shape. But she didn't type.

Not yet.

She opened her inbox instead. Her fingers moved slowly, not hesitating, just deliberate. She typed James's name into the search bar and waited. It didn't take long to find the message. It was short. Tidy. Efficient.

"I've got someone you might want to talk to. Knows a bit about the foundation. Reliable. Not too close. Plays it safe. You'll like him."

Her stomach clenched. She remembered the message now. She hadn't questioned it at the time. Felix had entered her world so seamlessly, like someone who'd been waiting just outside the frame. Helpful. Empathetic. Quiet.

Now it didn't feel like coincidence.

She reread the message, each word more clinical than the last. Reliable. Not too close. Plays it safe.

Her mind didn't jump to betrayal. Not yet. But the seed had been planted. And it settled in the hollows of her ribs like something growing teeth.

She clicked away from the email and opened a new document. This time, her hands didn't hesitate.

She began listing names. Events. Fragments. Half-memories she had dismissed. Quotes. Voices. Phrases from Felix. Expressions from James. She let them pile onto the page like evidence in a case no one else would believe. She saved it without a title, tucked it deep into a folder no one would think to open. She copied Ophelia's video files to a second drive. Then a third. One she taped into the lining of her coat. One she slipped between the mattress and her bedframe. The third she held in her palm for a long moment, unsure if she should hide it—or carry it like a blade.

Her hand trembled once. Only once.

She returned to her inbox and hovered over an old voicemail. One from James, one where he had told her she was not alone, where he had promised she did not have to carry the weight of it by herself.

She played it again.

The voice that filled the room was soft, warm, composed—steady in a way she had once clung to like a life raft. Yet through every gentle word, there was a silence too loud to ignore. He had never asked if she was sure. Not when she said Alexei needed to pay. Not when she began stitching together the pieces of her revenge. Not even when she said she wanted to confront him.

He had never told her to stop. He had only told her how to proceed.

A slow ache spread through her chest, tight and suffocating, not from certainty but from something darker—an unease she could not name, a quiet alarm ringing deep within her bones.

She opened her voice recorder and pressed record, her voice brittle and low.

"Day one," she said. "I found the voice. It was him. Felix. But now I think... I think maybe James knew more than he ever admitted. I think he pointed me in a direction and never once looked back."

She closed the laptop without ceremony and sat there, motionless, staring at the wall.

There were no tears. No screams. No breaking open.

Only silence, thick and unbearable, sinking into her until it filled every corner of her hollowed-out self.

Something was unraveling, slow and certain.

◇◇⬯◇◇⬯◇◇⬯

Chapter 36:

I *Was Poisoned*

The dusk that settled over Love's parents' house wasn't peaceful. It was the kind that held its breath. Nothing stirred. Even the curtains, normally swaying from the breeze that slithered through the cracks in the old windows, hung still tonight. The walls seemed to listen. The air hung heavier than usual—damp with anticipation, waiting for a match to be struck.

She had been sitting in the same chair for over an hour, barely moving, only shifting occasionally to unclench her jaw or release the pressure in her fists. Her nails had dug half-moon indents into her palms. A hoodie hung loosely from her shoulders, its sleeves pulled halfway over her hands, fingers twitching every few minutes. Her phone sat in front of her on the dining table, next to a glass of water she hadn't touched. The only thing that kept her tethered was the weight of the flash drive in her hand. It was small. Inconspicuous. But it might as well have been a landmine.

When the message lit up her screen, she didn't jump.

James: "You home? I can stop by."

She read it three times before responding. She didn't know what kind of version of him would be showing up. But she knew what she would be.

Love: "Come."

She didn't move after sending it. Just sat back, waiting. Preparing. The calm wasn't real. It was the kind that sat just before a storm cracked the sky in two. She could feel it in her chest.

Fifteen minutes later, headlights swept past the window. She heard the car door. Then the knock—two soft taps. Like he was being polite.

She opened the door before he could knock again. James stepped inside like he owned no guilt. His sleeves were rolled, his shirt crisp despite the hour. His expression was mild. Practiced. As if he thought casualness might soften the blow of everything he had kept from her.

"Hey," he said, cautiously. "You look tired."

Love didn't respond. She turned and walked toward the living room without a word. James followed, hesitating only briefly.

"Thought we could talk," he tried again. "It's been a while."

She sat down at the dining table again, letting the silence drag.

"You disappeared after the funeral," she finally said. "No call. No message. You didn't even ask what happened. Or what I lost."

He folded his arms across his chest. "I thought you needed space. You seemed like you were still trying to get your head on straight."

"That wasn't space," she said. "That was abandonment."

James sighed. "I didn't want to make things worse. You were fragile."

Her gaze lifted to his. "I was poisoned."

There was a beat of silence.

"Love, I was just trying to clear your name," he said. "Its not my fault you feel guilty for blood on your hands.."

She corrected him. "Blood on our hands. After all, didn't you serve as the murder cleanup crew? Trying to manipulate the outcome?"

His jaw tensed. "That's not fair."

"It's accurate," she replied. "You've been manipulating the outcome since the start. You handed me Felix and told me he was trustworthy. You made sure he looked safe. Familiar. You gave me poison and called it medicine."

James's nostrils flared slightly. "I gave you someone you could talk to. Someone removed enough to be objective."

"Objective?" she said, rising slowly from her seat. "You gave me Alexei's half-brother."

He hesitated. "I didn't think that mattered."

"You didn't think it mattered?" Her voice lifted slightly, incredulous. "You didn't think telling me that the man I was in love with, had a sibling embedded in my life who was serving me poison against him, was relevant?"

He raised a hand as if to defend himself, but before he could speak, she closed the distance between them and slapped him hard across the face.

The sound cracked in the room like thunder.

James reeled slightly, one hand to his cheek, eyes wide. "What the hell, Love?"

"That's for everything you didn't say."

He stepped back. "You're losing it."

She grabbed the collar of his shirt, shoved him backward into the nearest chair. He stumbled into it, palms catching the edge of the seat.

"You're going to watch what you've ignored," she said, already moving to the TV. She plugged in the flash drive. The screen blinked to life. The folder opened.

"Love, whatever this is—"

She didn't even look at him. "Shut up."

The first video began.

Ophelia appeared, hunched in a corner. Her eyes were glassy, her voice small, broken in a way that wasn't natural. Her hands twisted in her lap. The bruises on her neck peeked out from her sweater.

"I love him," she whispered. "He says we're gonna get married."

The screen flickered. She flinched. Off-camera, a voice spoke.

"Sit up, Ophelia. Now. Sit up, now! You know better."

James's body went stiff. His hands gripped the edge of the seat.

The second video played immediately. Ophelia was smaller. Quiet. Curled into herself like she was trying to disappear. When she spoke, it was as if she were mouthing lines someone had drilled into her skull.

"I said I'd be better. I won't cry. I said sorry. I said I'd be quiet—"

Then again: "Sit up, Ophelia."

Felix's voice. Calm. Measured. The same tone he'd used at Love's kitchen table when offering her peppermint tea.

When the screen finally faded to black, the silence in the room was sickening.

James leaned forward, elbows on his knees, face pale. "I didn't know he—"

She interrupted, her voice low. "You let me trust him."

"I thought he was helpi-"

"You didn't think. You cleaned up after me and didn't ask why. You stood in blood and called it closure."

His voice cracked. "You said you were sure. I trusted you."

"You wanted to trust me because it kept you clean," she said. "But it didn't keep me safe."

He stood, pacing now. "I didn't know he was capable of that. I didn't know he'd be in the video. You can't pin that on me."

She picked up the glass of water and hurled it across the room. It shattered against the wall, pieces skittering across the tile.

"You don't get to decide what's yours to carry. You gave me the weapon and told me to aim."

James stopped pacing. "I did what I thought was best. You needed someone, and Felix—he was reliable."

"He tortured her," she whispered. "He broke her until she whispered his name like a prayer."

James covered his face.

Love's voice was quieter now, but colder. "I was pregnant."

He looked up sharply.

Her expression didn't change. "I didn't tell anyone. Not even him. But I ended it. Because you convinced me he was a monster."

James looked like the floor had given out under him. "Oh, God. I thought you made that up to seem less suspicious."

"I thought I was protecting something innocent. I didn't know the real monster was standing behind me, applauding."

She stepped forward, grabbed the front of his shirt again. "Do you understand what you cost me?"

"I didn't mean—"

She punched him.

Not hard enough to knock him down, but enough to make him stumble. She hit him again, fists against his chest, against his shoulder. She shoved him, kicked the chair he'd sat in.

"You watched me burn. You poured gasoline and called it guidance."

James didn't stop her. He just covered his face, breathing hard.

She stepped back, chest rising and falling with fury.

"If you tell Felix any of this," she said, voice deadly calm, "I will carve your name into the walls of my grief and feed it to the dogs."

James blinked. All he could manage was "I'm sorry."

"You think I'm unraveling?" she said. "I haven't even begun. But if you so much as whisper this to him—I will find you. And I will feast on what's left."

The room buzzed with silence.

James moved toward the door slowly, like every step might be a landmine.

Before he stepped outside of the door frame, she laughed menacingly and said "You lost your sister, too..that's why you mumbled karma the night you called me...Maybe, it was."

He didn't turn around. He couldn't. He forced his feet out and left.

And Love stood in the center of the wreckage.

Finally, alone. Ready.

Felix was next.

Chapter 37:

*Y*ou Shouldn't Have Left Her Alone

The house was too quiet, but not in the way quiet should be. It was the sort of silence that pressed against the walls, as if the air itself was holding its breath, waiting for something to crack. The furniture stood too still. The floorboards made no noise beneath her bare feet. Even her mother's soft movements in the kitchen felt distant, like the soundtrack to someone else's life. Love didn't speak much anymore, not to Dahlia, not to Ashton, not even to herself. She just existed—drifting from room to room, pretending to sleep, pretending to eat, pretending she hadn't destroyed her life in pursuit of a truth that might've never been real to begin with.

After the shooting, she'd only come home to silence her parents' concerns, convinced it would just be temporary. She had planned to move out and get her own place, one not tainted with her crimes. She never unpacked. Never organized. Never bothered checking the mail. The envelopes had piled up on the sideboard in the front hallway—some opened, most not, all quietly ignored by parents too polite to throw away what wasn't theirs. And that Tuesday morning, Love was only near the pile because she was looking for a pen.

She spotted it by accident—a plain white envelope, tucked halfway beneath a stack of expired flyers and old utility bills. Her name was written across the front in handwriting that was too sharp, too angry, too male to be hers. There was no return address.

Her breath caught.

She recognized the scrawl immediately. It belonged to the detective she'd once screamed at in a police station hallway, a man whose face she'd nearly clawed open in desperation. She'd begged him for an unredacted version of

Ophelia's autopsy, demanding something—anything—that hadn't been filtered through bureaucratic indifference. He had promised to send her what he could. She'd assumed he never followed through. She'd assumed James got to it first. But it had been here. All this time. Waiting.

Her hands trembled as she tore the envelope open and slid out the folded report. The paper felt heavier than it should have—weighted with something irreversible. She didn't need to scan long. Her eyes landed on the same line she had once seen from James's copy, but this time, the timestamp made her knees buckle.

Fetal tissue detected. Approx. 6–8 weeks gestation.

Information withheld from public disclosure per internal discretion.

This report was dated long before the shooting. It wasn't a leak from James's insider network. It wasn't something handed off in the shadows. This had been official. This had been hers. Meant for her.

It had simply arrived while she was gone.

She hadn't been living here when it came—she'd been too busy spiraling through grief and fury, crashing on couches, avoiding mirrors, digging through Alexei's every move like a woman chasing ghosts. The envelope had landed in a house that no longer felt like hers, and no one had thought to mention it. No one had dared touch her name.

She folded the paper back slowly, carefully, her thumb pressed into the crease like she could pin time in place. It wasn't just the content that made her stomach cave in. It was the timing. If she had received it when it was sent, if she'd been here, things would have been different.

With that knowledge in hand, she would've returned to the detective. She would've demanded more. Would've asked about DNA—whether any samples had been collected. Would've insisted they test for paternity. She would've taken Alexei's toothbrush, his hairbrush, a napkin from his coffee table. Anything. She would've approached him with the clinical urgency of a woman searching for facts—not the rage of someone ready to kill.

But that's not how it happened.

Because the information didn't reach her in time, the cracks filled in with speculation. And speculation, fed by grief and fear and James's whispering mouth, hardened into belief. She had believed Alexei was guilty because no one gave her reason to question it.

If she had opened that envelope earlier, she would've had questions instead of a sentence. Doubt instead of a trigger. A test instead of a death.

Maybe he still would've died.

Maybe the truth would've caught up with him eventually.

But what haunted her even more was the realization that she hadn't needed much convincing. That some part of her had been so primed to doubt him, so raw and ravenous for someone to blame, that she hadn't stopped long enough to consider what it would mean if he was telling the truth. She hadn't asked. She hadn't paused. She had listened to fear instead of her own instincts.

But not like that.

Not with his mouth stained red, saying her name like a prayer.

She slid the paper back into the envelope and stared at the dining room wall. Her chest felt like it had been hollowed out with a dull blade. But the tears didn't come. Not anymore. Crying was for people who still thought someone might come running.

◇◇ ◇◇

That night, she didn't sleep. She plugged in the USB drive again—the same one she had watched before. She knew every second of it now. She didn't need to hear Ophelia's voice. It was the other voice she was listening for.

The one that spoke in commands. In cold, familiar syllables.

Felix.

She let the screen run to black and stared at the reflection of her own face in the glass. She didn't look like someone in mourning. She looked like someone who had outlived the part of her meant to survive.

He had watched Ophelia break. He had documented her unraveling, trapped her like a moth behind glass, and then moved on to the next. He had walked into Love's grief with soft eyes and steady hands, spoon-fed her comfort, and sat across from her like he wasn't the architect of her sister's final months.

He hadn't just tricked her. He had rewritten her grief.

Love sat at the edge of her bed and opened her notebook. This wasn't for reflection. This was for strategy.

She wrote down everything. Patterns. Timelines. Phrases he had used. The way he always knew when to leave. The way he never pushed but always lingered. The way he had watched her the day she killed Alexei, and said nothing. As if he knew it was already done.

He had underestimated her.

She picked up her phone and sent a text:

Come over tonight. Eleven.

It was vague. Innocent enough to be taken at face value. But not to Felix.

To Felix, it meant opportunity.

His reply came within seconds.

I'll be there.

She didn't smile. Didn't move.

When she looked at her reflection again, she didn't see a victim.

She saw what came after.

◇◇⌐ ◇◇⌐ ◇?⌐ ◇?⌐ ◇?⌐

Chapter 38:

The Quiet Arrangement

Love stared at her phone, watching the Clock App's dial moving slowly. Sitting in the stillness of that waiting hour, the reality of what she'd set in motion pressed down like a closing jaw. She wasn't waiting to talk. She wasn't even waiting to be heard. She was waiting to see something bleed through his mask. She needed to know what his silence sounded like in a room with no witnesses. She needed to see the edges of his composure fray under lamplight and grief. The kind of grief he couldn't fake convincingly. The kind he'd never earned. Not to accuse. Not to beg. But to watch him closely and confirm what she had been trying not to believe. The hours stretched long and quiet, her breath thin in her chest, as she stared at the untouched mug on the counter.

What lingered now was not uncertainty, but a gnawing sense of inevitability.

Her nerves didn't jitter. They dulled. Her skin felt like it no longer fit quite right. The house had never been this still.

Or maybe it had—but tonight, she noticed every inch of it suffocating her. It was past eleven, and she didn't need to explain. She knew Felix Sinclair would come. There was something about him that only stirred after hours, when the world quieted and grief made people soft. Maybe he thought she was becoming one of them. Maybe he came to see it.

He knocked twice. The sound wasn't hesitant or demanding—it was measured, composed, too perfectly timed. Her heart didn't skip a beat; it sank instead, as if bracing for something she already knew. For a moment she stood there, hand hovering over the doorknob, staring at the wood like it might splinter open without her. Every inch of her body was aware of what stood on the other side. When she finally turned the handle, it wasn't out of curiosity. It was confirmation. She opened the door without speaking and stepped aside. He entered as if the space already belonged to him. Love didn't look at him. She walked barefoot across the tiled floor, her cardigan slipping off one shoulder, too loose to care. The living room smelled like cinnamon tea and antiseptic. Two mugs were steeping. One for the performance.

"I wasn't sure you'd come," she said, barely above a whisper, eyes fixed on the steam curling upward from the mugs.

"You asked. I came," he replied.

No smile. No warmth. His coat still damp from the rain. He removed it neatly, placed it on the back of the chair, and sat across from her like it was a transaction. She slid a mug toward him but didn't touch her own.

"I lost the baby," she said. It didn't sound like grief. It sounded like inventory. As if she were recounting something misplaced, not something buried. Her eyes didn't lift. Her voice remained even, emptied of sentiment. Felix didn't react, not in any visible way. He held her gaze a second too long, then nodded.

"I'm sorry."

"You already knew, didn't you?" she asked, her voice level. He didn't deny it immediately. His stillness said more than words.

"James told you?" A pause. Not too long. Just enough for her to know he was crafting the answer.

"I assumed," he finally said. "Based on... everything."

"Because of how things unfolded," she murmured. He didn't answer.

"You're not surprised," she added, eyes finally rising to meet his. "Why not?"

Felix tilted his head slightly. "I didn't know what you'd do."

"No," she said quietly. "But you were hoping I'd break." He didn't respond. She let the silence press against them like wet cloth, heavy and suffocating.

"You're not sleeping," he observed after too long.

"I haven't slept properly since before he died." He nodded. Said nothing else.

She stood then, slowly, like the act cost her something. "Thank you for coming."

"That's all?" he asked, looking at her too closely.

194

"Yes."

He lingered, only a moment. Then he rose, adjusted his scarf, and picked up his coat.

"I'm around," he said, stepping toward the door.

"I know."

He didn't try to touch her. Didn't offer sympathy. Didn't stay. She closed the door after him and stood in the silence, her back against the wood, until the cold settled into her spine. That night, she didn't sleep.

She arrived at the Brunswell Archive just after 9 a.m. She had registered herself weeks ago under a fabricated name—Dr. Eliza Rahmani, a graduate researcher studying behavioral ethics under a defunct European grant. The ID badge worked. The system didn't question her. The receptionist smiled without really seeing her and printed the access pass without a second glance.

Inside, the building was a monument to sterile erasure. White flooring, motion-activated lights, glass-paneled conference rooms that hadn't been used in years. It smelled of ozone and polished metal, like science scrubbed clean of history. She walked past display plaques of philanthropic partnerships and staged humanitarian grants. Each felt like a curtain drawn across something festering. The real research wasn't out here in the open. It never was.

She took the elevator to the lower level, where the archives held restricted files. No colorful signage. No helpful staff. Just silence, and a metal corridor lined with filing cabinets and access terminals. The lights flickered awake one by one as she moved forward. She found the drawer. APH-243 / ER6. The lock was already disengaged, the drawer slightly misaligned—as if it had been opened recently but not carefully. She pulled it slowly, and the smell of old paper and oxidized staples reached her before the folder even came into view.

It was beige. Faded. A folder like any other. But the weight of it hit her chest before she even touched it. She opened it. The first page was a log sheet. Clinical handwriting. Multiple entries. The initials F.S. repeated down the column.

She turned the page. Blank consent form. Then a patient intake file. No real name. Only Subject 243. Then, halfway down, typed in bold under "Alias": Oph G. Her lungs seized. The world narrowed to the sound of the paper against her fingers and the flicker of overhead light. She flipped to the next page. Then the next. And then she saw it:

Week 2: Induction Phase

Subject 243 began displaying measurable affective reactivity. Test modules involved direct exposure to emotionally triggering stimuli—video clips featuring family events, distorted audio messages voiced by siblings, fabricated diary entries with inconsistencies designed to incite distress. Subject exhibited multiple crying episodes and brief dissociative responses during familial playback trials. Sedation introduced following escalation.

Week 3: Operant Conditioning

Behavioral compliance testing began. Positive reinforcement was inconsistently delivered—brief periods of companionship, access to calming stimuli—while non-compliance triggered sensory deprivation protocols. Subject was confined in isolation chambers for durations of 4 to 6 hours, with sound and light removed entirely. Audio cues triggered compliance in subsequent trials, suggesting effective behavioral reprogramming.

Week 4: Dissociative Threshold Studies

Subject exposed to cognitive interference tests involving simultaneous auditory and visual contradictions while prompted to recall painful memories. Heart rate variability noted as elevated. Skin conductance spikes during maternal recall prompts. Dissociative indicators recorded in 70% of sessions. Subject began referring to self in third person. Researchers marked this as "encouraging."

Week 5: Physiological Decline

Medical readings indicated 12.6% body weight reduction since Week 1. Blood panels showed vitamin deficiencies, consistent with calorie restriction and stress-induced absorption issues. Sleep study noted REM suppression and micro-awakenings every 13 minutes. Subject exhibited signs of dehydration, light sensitivity, and minor tremors. Intervention was denied. Log note: "Condition manageable. Continue."

Week 6: Withdrawal Attempt

Subject verbally requested termination of participation. Notes indicated vocal distress, pacing, visible tremors. Request denied. Surveillance increased. Communication with outside contacts suspended. Subject became increasingly compliant. Noted to display low speech volume, minimal eye contact. Log note: "Behavior normalized. No further threats of disruption expected."

Margin annotation—rushed, cramped: **Termination not authorized. Monitor only. No contact.**

Love stared at the words. The folder didn't just confirm what she feared—it revealed what they had never even thought to hide. It hadn't been therapy. It hadn't even been a mistake. It had been deliberate. She turned the page and found signatures. One after another. Felix Sinclair. Each initial. Each timestamp. Each endorsement.

He hadn't just watched. He had conducted it. Photograph after photograph of brain scans. Emotional reactivity charts. Side notes in mechanical language—about her sister's "maladaptive attachment response," her "hyper-reactivity to loss stimuli," her "rejection of narrative restructuring."

She didn't scream. She didn't cry. She took her phone out and began photographing each page. One by one. Carefully. Systematically. She uploaded them to a burner account. Saved them to a drive. Created a mirror backup. She knew how this worked. She wasn't going to be erased like her sister.

She returned the folder exactly as she found it. Then she sat on the floor, her back against the wall, and closed her eyes for what felt like hours. Her mind played every memory she had of Ophelia like a corrupted tape—glitches where meaning used to be.

The late nights. The skipped meals. The screaming matches when she wasn't allowed to go out. How she'd shake when Love tried to touch her arm. How she'd laugh too loudly and then go silent for hours. The bruises no one asked about. The notebooks filled with strange patterns and fragments of words.

They thought it was teenage rebellion. A mental spiral. They told her to eat. To sleep. To stop being dramatic. But it had been all of this. And he had done it.

She finally stood. Her body felt distant from her. Her hands no longer hers. She walked out of the archive and didn't look back. She didn't cry in the car. But she didn't drive home either. She sat in the lot for nearly an hour, staring at her own reflection in the rearview mirror. The girl who looked back at her was hollow-eyed, lips pale, hands clenched around something invisible.

When she arrived home, the house felt wrong. Too quiet. Too warm. Too normal. She didn't go inside. She opened the photo folder again and stared at the words: Monitor only. No contact. Her sister had begged to leave. They made her stay. They tore her down and called it progress. And Felix had signed every line.

The grief in her chest shifted. Hardened. Took shape. She was done asking questions. Thursday wasn't about mourning anymore. It was about correction. And some things? Some things didn't deserve to be buried.

Chapter 39 – Part I:

The Invitation

The building no longer had a name. Once, it might have held titles, documents, or decisions that shaped lives. Now, it held silence. Love chose it for that reason—a silence that devours echoes, that absorbs everything and gives nothing back.

She stood in the center of the room like a forgotten hymn sharpened into steel. The ceiling hung low, the beams ribbed and rusting. Filing cabinets lined the walls like coffins left ajar, papers long devoured by time. A single lamp flickered above her, casting shadows that swayed like ghosts too tired to leave.

She had the folder in her coat. The wire in her hand. And something ancient, bitter, and wordless clenched between her teeth.

Not yet. Not until it would matter most.

She had laid the trap with precision. Fishing line strung through the ruins, looping behind cabinets, threaded through cabinet handles, tied beneath gauze and mildew. It was nothing to look at. But it would hold. And it would hurt.

When the door creaked open, she did not move. She only listened.

Felix entered dressed in black. Not mourning black. Not the jagged shade of guilt. But the ceremonial kind. A silence worn by men who believe they are above consequence. His coat was clean. His jaw freshly shaven. His breath did not quicken. His eyes adjusted to the dark as though it bowed to him.

"This is dramatic," he murmured. "But then again, so are you."

She remained still. Her silence tightened the room.

"You wanted to talk," he continued. "Though I see now, this is more a final act."

She turned slowly. Her voice, when it came, was colder than the rot in the walls.

"I read everything."

His smile flickered. Not in shame. In pleasure.

"You went to the archive?"

"I saw your notes. The trials. The experiments. The pregnancy results. The reports. The lies etched into clinical language."

He tilted his head like a scholar hearing a familiar theory.

"And?"

"Say her name."

He did not. He smiled wider.

"She was pliable," he said. "Beautiful in how easily she bent. You tried to save her. You mistook fragility for innocence. That was your mistake."

"She was *eighteen*."

"She was receptive."

"You *violated* her."

He did not flinch.

"I loved her. I gave her something sacred. I gave her attention."

"She was pregnant."

"She wanted that," he said softly, like a confession meant for a mirror. "We spoke of futures. She asked if we'd marry. If I'd stay. Her dreams were foolish. But earnest."

"She died believing you loved her."

"She lived as proof of it."

Love stepped forward.

"You drugged her. Watched her unravel. You turned her pain into data. Labeled her screams."

"She needed someone to see her fall."

"You killed her."

"I immortalized her."

"She begged to leave."

"She was a flame," he said. "She would've gone out in the wind. I kept her burning."

Love pulled out the folder. Her hand shook with the weight of it.

"Subject attempted unauthorized contact with family. Risk of exposure increased. Recommend immediate lockdown. Signed: F.Sinclair."

"She called me," she whispered. "She tried to come home."

"She panicked. She would've destroyed everything. I preserved her."

"You *raped* her."

"She sobbed for it. She needed someone to claim her. You saw the footage. She wanted to belong."

"She wanted to be free."

"No," he said, stepping closer. "She wanted to be remembered."

Love's voice dropped.

"She died with your name on her lips."

"She lived with mine in her blood."

Her fist cut through the air.

The slap cracked like a faultline. He staggered, caught the table. Blood kissed his lips.

He laughed.

"There it is. The fury. The inheritance."

She struck again. Her fist crashed into his cheekbone. He fell, groaned, still grinning.

"Let's talk about you," he rasped. "The girl who pulled the trigger on a man who would've bled for her. You didn't pause. Didn't question. You obeyed."

"I thought—"

"You didn't think. You hunted. You followed grief like it was gospel. And when he begged, when he choked on your name, you walked away."

Her throat closed.

"You aborted the child like it was rot. Like his blood was too heavy to carry."

She stumbled. Her breath cracked. Then came the scream. Feral. Marrow-deep. A sound made of knives and aftermath.

"SHUT UP."

She lunged. Fists met flesh. His blood ran in arcs across the wall. He coughed, teeth red, still laughing.

"Go on," he gasped. "Destroy me. It won't unmake what you are."

She slammed his skull into the floor. Her hands hovered over his throat. She trembled. But she did not kill him.

She reached for the wire.

She pulled.

Felix gasped as his arms wrenched backward. Ligaments strained. Wire cinched tight, cutting through his composure.

He writhed, panting, and then he laughed again. It was quieter now. Crooked. Almost fond.

"You mourn him like he was some kind of saint," he said. "But your beloved Alexei? He was not a martyr. He was the cleanup crew."

She froze.

"He didn't recommend her for the program," Felix said, voice slick with mockery, every word curdled with amusement. "He found out. Poor Alexei. Always a little too late. Always thinking he could tear a body from the jaws of the beast after the blood was already drying."

Love shook her head, but Felix barely noticed. He watched her the way a snake watches something it has already swallowed.

"He tried," Felix said, the corners of his bloodstained mouth lifting. "Sabotaged the tests. Delayed the protocols. Flailed like a drowning man, thinking his thrashing mattered to the tide."

Her vision blurred, but he kept talking, his voice steady, merciless, almost tender.

"He thought he could save her," Felix said, as if it were the punchline to a very old joke. "Thought he could drag her out and carry her back to you, still breathing. Thought he could rewrite the story without staining his pretty hands."

Love's breath hitched violently.

"You never even asked him," Felix said, and this time his voice lowered, velvet and lethal. "You never let him explain. You never looked him in the eye. You stood there with a bullet trembling in your hands and a question rotting in your throat, and you chose silence. You chose rage. You chose James, because he made it easier to hate than to think."

"Shut up," she gasped, but it came out thin, breakable.

Felix's grin widened, splitting his face into something grotesque.

"You killed him," he whispered. "You slaughtered the only man who was still fool enough to believe you were worth salvaging."

Her hands were shaking now, her nails digging crescent moons into her palms so deep she felt the skin break.

"You don't know anything," she snapped, but it was already too late; the ground beneath her was gone.

"I know you better than he ever did," Felix said. "I know what you are. I saw it the first time you looked at me and didn't flinch."

She stumbled back, fighting for breath she could not catch.

"You made me," she screamed, voice raw, splintered.

"I didn't make you," Felix said, smiling with a terrible softness. "I just peeled away the parts of you that lied about what you were."

Tears blurred her vision, but she blinked them back furiously.

"You ruined everything!" she spat. "You ruined her—"

"I liberated her," Felix interrupted, voice almost reverent. "She didn't have to live long enough to become what you are now."

Love's entire body trembled, but he wasn't finished.

"You think you became a monster because of me," Felix said. "But you always had the hunger. You always wanted to bleed something dry. I just gave you a mirror to watch yourself."

He stepped closer, so slowly, so mockingly patient.

"You didn't kill Alexei because you had to," he said, voice dropping to a low hum. "You killed him because it felt good."

"That's not true," she whispered.

Felix chuckled darkly, a sound like rot peeling from old walls.

"It is," he said. "You just don't want to admit it."

He leaned down, eyes gleaming with madness, with worship, with possession.

"You were my greatest creation," he said. "And you didn't even need coaxing."

Love stared at him, the truth splintering inside her like glass under a hammer.

She was not fighting to stay human.

She was fighting to deny what she had already become.

She exhaled.

It did not sound like breathing. It sounded like something escaping—a pressure long held under the ribs, a breaking of a dam that had lived inside her for years. The air seemed to change around her, thickening, humming against the walls, and when the first rat appeared, she almost wasn't surprised.

They came the way rot does: quietly at first, seeping through cracks, rising from the forgotten places where light had never dared linger. She heard them before she saw them, the faint tremor of claws against stone, the wet shuffling of bodies moving as one. Not summoned. Not called. Just drawn, as if the truth made flesh was too loud to ignore.

Felix saw them only when the first claws sank into his flesh.

One latched onto his leg, biting through cloth and skin as if neither mattered. Another scurried up his side, its teeth finding the tender hollow beneath his ribs. He jerked against the wires binding him, a wild, panicked thrashing that only deepened the cuts. His scream tore free then, high and desperate, a sound so raw it seemed to strip the very air apart.

Love watched, her hands loose at her sides, her heart silent. She felt no satisfaction, no triumph. What unfurled inside her was colder, deeper, something that had no name. It was not cruelty. It was not mercy. It was simply the truth of him, peeled open before her like an offering.

The rats swarmed him, their bodies slick and glistening, their teeth small and cruel. They worked with a purpose almost holy, shredding fabric, carving through skin, burrowing into muscle. His body became a canvas of ruin. Blood sprayed across the floor in thick, sick splatters. His shrieks pitched higher, then broke into wet, choking gasps as they tore him down, layer by layer.

Somewhere in the distance of her mind, Love felt the part of her that should have recoiled, should have cried out, fall silent and still. It watched alongside her, detached, fascinated, hollow. She realized, with a strange kind of mourning, that the girl who would have wept for him had already died before the rats ever arrived.

She crouched beside him, her shadow falling over the ruin of him. The rats parted around her legs without hesitation, as if they recognized her not as an intruder but as something born of the same hunger.

"Look at me," she said.

Felix turned his head with what little strength he had left. His eyes were wide, glassy, drowning. His mouth opened in a soft, broken noise that might once have been a plea.

"You do not get to die," she said, voice steady as a blade being drawn. "Death would be a kindness you don't deserve. You stay here. You stay with yourself."

She pulled out her phone and pressed record. Her thumb was precise. Her breath came slow and even.

"Subject Number 243-B," she said, voice clinical, detached. "Male. Age thirty-two. Initial exposure to sensory invasion prompted immediate vocal escalation, degradation of coherence, loss of motor control, and rapid systemic collapse."

Felix sobbed through blood, his chest shuddering, but she stepped through the growing pools of red without pause.

"Subject exhibits persistent delusions of grandeur. Believes suffering heightens significance. Displays confusion at the notion that pain diminishes, rather than exalts."

She crouched lower, until her mouth brushed the ragged meat of his ear.

"This," she whispered, "is what it feels like to be taken apart. This is what it feels like to be nothing but a study. To have your agony catalogued like a footnote no one will ever read."

He moaned, a soft, broken sound more animal than human.

"Note," she murmured into the ruined shell of him, "Subject remained conscious throughout full systemic evisceration."

She saved the file. Named it: *For O.*

Only then, as she rose to her feet, did she add one final line, her voice barely more than a breath above the gnashing of teeth:

"Final observation: Subject, once a god in his own mind, ended small enough to fit inside the belly of a rat."

She stepped back. The door swung closed behind her, the sound deep and final, like a tomb sealing itself from the living world.

Love did not turn back.

She did not pray.

She did not weep.

The girl she had been would have....

But that girl had been eaten long before Felix ever bared his teeth. Now, in the cold dark, the truth had finally finished its meal.

❖❖❖❖❖❖❖❖❖❖❖❖❖❖❖❖

Chapter 39 - Part II:

I *Set The Wolf On Fire*

The world outside the windshield blurred until it became something shapeless and broken, a river of color bleeding itself empty. The engine hummed beneath her like a body still fighting for breath, but inside her chest there was only silence, a low, aching quiet that stretched until it filled her ribs and pressed against her throat. Her hands clung to the wheel, too tightly, blood dried into the creases of her palms, the stains sinking so deep it felt like they had always been there. Even when she loosened her fingers, she could feel it—the ghost of him—threaded through her skin.

The road twisted along the cliffs, the ocean crashing in the distance like something old and furious, and she did not notice when the car drifted to a stop. She sat there with the headlights pointed at the endless dark, listening to the rain tap against the roof, the salt-heavy wind clawing through the crack in the window, threading cold fingers into her hair, into her mouth, into the hollow places she could no longer protect.

The silence inside the car grew heavier, pulling at her bones, a silence so full it felt like it had weight, like it had teeth. She looked into the rearview mirror and saw a face she did not know, skin pale, eyes rimmed with red, a stranger molded from grief and ash.

The phone burned in her hand. She pressed the call button with the same instinct she might have used to close a wound with her own teeth. When James answered, she did not greet him.

"She's gone," she said, her voice cracking apart like dry wood under too much weight. "The girl who waited. The girl who still believed."

The line crackled with his breath, but no words came at first. He let the silence stretch, let it scrape against her ears, let it hollow out the space between them until nothing was left but the weight of what she had done.

"Was it worth it?" he asked.

Love closed her eyes. The air in her lungs tasted like rust.

She almost laughed.

Almost.

"No," she said.

And for a moment, the world held still, like it was listening.

"No, but it was necessary."

The words sat between them, a monument they could not tear down.

James exhaled, soft and broken.

"Your parents have been calling. They're afraid something's happened."

Love let the words roll past her. They felt like they belonged to a different lifetime, spoken by strangers to someone she no longer knew how to be.

"Tell them," she said, voice raw, "Love is dead."

The words dropped between them like a body. She ended the call before he could answer.

◇◇◇◇

The rain softened to mist, and the night exhaled, and somewhere beyond the cliffs the waves grew quieter, retreating from the world as if even they no longer wanted to bear witness. She sat there until the sky grew pale and colorless, until the horizon blurred into a smudge of gray. Then she turned the car toward home.

The house welcomed her with nothing but silence.

The door swung open without resistance.

Her coat fell where it slipped from her shoulders, puddling on the floor like another body left behind.

Her boots dragged streaks of water and blood across the hardwood, a broken map of the places she had been.

The hallway smelled wrong. Like detergent that could not cover up the scent of abandonment.

She reached the kitchen. Turned the faucet until it screamed. The water poured out cold and violent and endless. She dropped to her knees and shoved her hands beneath it, scrubbing, harder and harder, until her skin burned. The blood refused to lift. It clung to her like memory, like consequence, like all the things that no one had ever been able to wash away.

She scrubbed until her fingers bled, until the pads of her skin went numb.

She scrubbed until her throat tightened with the effort not to scream.

The door opened behind her. She did not hear it.

Footsteps crossed the floor. Breath caught and stumbled. Her mother's voice was the first thing to break.

"Love."

A whisper. A prayer. A name that had already stopped belonging to the thing kneeling at the sink.

Her father moved slower. Stopped when he saw her. Did not speak.

Love stared at the running water. Her body shook with the violence of trying to stay whole.

"It won't come off," she whispered. The words scraped raw against the inside of her mouth. "I've tried. I've tried so hard."

Her mother collapsed beside her, gathering her into shaking arms. Her father knelt behind them, silent and broken. Together they tried to hold her upright, but Love's body was a puppet with no strings, slumping between them, heavier than it should have been.

"I fixed it," she said. "I made it matter."

She pressed her forehead against her mother's shoulder, the fabric soaking up the salt of her breath, the fever of her skin.

"I gave her peace," she said, voice breaking. "I gave her something real. I gave her teeth."

Her father's hand found her back. His palm was shaking.

"I am not the daughter who cried wolf," she said, voice rising slightly, cracking open like a fault line. "I am the daughter who set the wolf on fire."

Her mother sobbed into her hair. Her father pressed his forehead to her spine. They were trying to anchor her. They were trying to keep her from floating away.

But they were too late.

She lifted her face and looked at them.

Eyes blown wide, rimmed with something worse than grief.

"I did it," she said.

The words tumbled from her mouth like teeth.

"I got justice."

The smile that followed was not human.

It was the smile of a body remembering what it once was before it was broken.

It was the smile of a thing that had finally stopped fighting the current pulling it under.

She collapsed into her mother's arms, and for a long, long moment, no one breathed.

They held her like a lifeline they could not hold onto, clutching her tighter as if she might slip through their fingers like smoke. But Love was already gone. The thing they were holding was only the echo.

They admitted her in silence. She did not fight. She did not speak. Her body moved because they moved it. Her hands folded where they were placed. Her mouth hung open, too tired even for protest.

The doctors whispered over her like priests preparing a body for burial.

They said her mind had folded inward. They said the damage was deep. They said it had not come all at once, but slowly, the way a cliff face erodes under the steady, patient pressure of the tide.

She offered no resistance as they strapped her to the gurney. She let them roll her down the hallway without a word.

The lights buzzed overhead, cold and white and endless. The walls smelled of bleach and sorrow. Every step they took carried her farther from herself.

One light flickered. Then another.

When the third flickered, her lips moved, just once.

"Don't let the lights flicker," she whispered. "That's when the rats come."

The nurse stiffened at her side, but Love had already closed her eyes.

Her body softened into vacancy, and her breath slowed.

She didn't flinch, nor did she dream.

Love was not lost.

She was taken, piece by piece, until there was nothing left to call back.

◈ ◈ ◈ ◈ ◈ ◈ ◈ ◈ ◈

Chapter 40:

W hat Love Could Not Survive

The walls were white in a way that punished, a sterile, merciless kind of white that stripped away names, memories, the shape of who you used to be. It was the white found inside broken bodies and forgotten tombs, the color that erased everything except the ache. Love sat in a chair that refused to move, her body folding into itself without urgency, without resistance. Her wrists dangled from her knees, her fingers curled slightly inward, as if the act of trembling had long ago been deemed unnecessary. The window was sealed shut with thick glass, framing a world that still stirred with wind and skeletal trees, but the air outside would never reach her. She was part of another ecosystem now, one where breath was an afterthought and time crawled so slowly it almost disappeared.

They called it a recovery ward. They used the word the way someone might speak to the dead, hoping that if they said it often enough, it might become true. But there was no recovery here, only observation, only the slow crumbling of a girl who had outlived all the names they had tried to bury her with. She was not a patient. She was not even broken in a way they understood. She was a thing kept between breath and silence, catalogued carefully but never really seen. They did not meet her eyes. They did not call her Love. She was Miss Godfrey, Patient 2709B, a girl with no pulse in her stare and no heat left in her skin.

She spoke once, her voice scraping from her throat like something pried loose from under stone. A nurse adjusting the IV line had paused just long enough for the words to slip out.

"Don't let the lights flicker," she said, quiet and certain, "that's when the rats come."

The nurse had smiled, a brittle thing that did not touch her eyes, and wrote the words down on a clipboard with clinical detachment. Delusional. Paranoid. Trauma-fused perception. No one asked her what she meant. They stopped meeting her gaze after that.

Her parents visited three days after she was admitted. Her mother carried a bouquet of daisies so bright they looked violent under the humming fluorescents. Her father's face had collapsed into itself, his hands shaking as he tried to clutch hers in a way that felt less like comfort and more like a plea. Love did not resist their touch. She simply let them exist beside her without acknowledging the noise they made, her eyes wandering past their faces as if searching for a memory that had long since faded. She did not cry. She did not flinch. She simply sat, a body that had once been a girl, now hollowed out into something no one knew how to hold.

James never came. His absence was its own kind of violence, sharper than any blow, more final than any betrayal. Rumors clung to the edges of the ward like mold. Airport sightings. Foreign cities. Hushed conversations behind closed doors. In the end, none of it mattered. His absence had already been sewn into her skin like thread through a wound that refused to close.

They offered her documents to sign, exit strategies, carefully worded hopes of future redemption. She did not lift the pencil. She stared at the papers the way a drowned woman might stare at the surface of the water she could never reach again.

There were no charges. No trial. No clean resolution for the world to pin to her chest. She had not confessed. She had not denied. She had simply arrived with her hands stained in memory and waited for them to decide what her silence meant.

They gave her a pencil instead of a pen, as if softer graphite might somehow dull the sharpness inside her. She wrote because there was nothing else left to do. She wrote under the flickering lights, her fingers dark with dust, her nails cracked and bleeding, the pages curling under the relentless pressure of her grief. She did not write apologies. She did not write explanations. She wrote because her body needed somewhere to put the rot growing inside her bones.

Some nights she sat at the window, her forehead pressed against the glass, rocking slowly back and forth as if trying to summon an old prayer. Some nights she laughed, a sound that startled even herself, thin and hysterical, a broken, high-pitched giggle that scraped out of her throat like a rusted hinge swinging open. It came at nothing and at everything—the walls, the lights, the smell of bleach, the sound of her own breathing. It bubbled up from places she had forgotten how to close off.

Some nights her hands turned against her. She clawed at them, dug her nails into the soft meat between her fingers, desperate to rip away the betrayal written into them, the betrayal that had pulled the trigger, that had signed away a life not yet born, that had stained her in ways no scrubbing would ever erase. The nurses noted the agitation on their charts. Behavioral disturbance. Emotional regression. Quiet recommendations for more sedation whispered in corners they thought she could not hear.

She heard everything.

She remembered everything.

The nights she walked home with blood stiffening under her fingernails.

The phone call where James had asked her if it had been worth it.

The sound of her own voice, answering in silence because no word had ever been enough.

She wrote it now. Not with hope, or defiance, only with the final weight of a truth too heavy to carry inside her any longer. Every word she carved into the paper was a prayer made of broken teeth. Every page she filled was a slow, brutal dissection of what remained of her.

She was not healing. She was not searching for forgiveness.

She was building her grave one sentence at a time.

It would not be soft, or beautiful. It would be hers.

The Final Entry

They would find it days after she stopped writing. Folded between two worn pages in a graphite-smudged notebook. No explanation. No date. No signature. Just this:

This is not a confession.
It is a resurrection of the ruin I became—
told for the saints, the sinners, and the ones still bleeding.
I fell in love.
I confessed that love with caution,
with trembling breath,
with my bare tongue pressed against the altar of his name.
In return, I was baptized in humiliation.
I lost my compass in the curve of his smile.
I became madness in a woman's body—
a wanderer with no map but the shadow of his voice.
In his love, I unraveled.
I turned chaos into currency,
traded it for touch,
and woke up drowning in catastrophe.
Scars no longer bleed,
but they itch like they still want to be remembered.
I knew the sound of his arrival
by the way the air shifted—
how silence stepped aside for him.
I recognized his footsteps
like they had been carved into my ribcage.
And I remember the silence of his departure
more clearly than any goodbye.
So much time has passed.
Still, I long to see him again—
the man I bled dry
and buried beneath the weight of my own fury.
Listen to my yearns.
My sobs.
My apologies whispered into doorways that no longer open.
I fell in love.

I dreamt of the white dress.
I rehearsed our vows like prayers.
I offered my soul as a balm to his wounds,
so he would not have to carry them alone.
My loyalty was not earned.
It was gifted—
like a lamb walking willingly into the fire.
My world lived inside the oceans of his eyes.
My hope sat cradled in the fragile glass of his hands.
He heard the things I didn't know how to say.
He became the home I was never meant to afford.
So listen now—
not to the woman I was,
but to the ruin I became.
Listen to my prayers
turned punishments.
I fell in love.
I wrapped that love in red tape,
knotted it in barbed wire,
offered it up like penance
to a God who longer believed in me.
I fell in love...
And Love died in the end.

In Memory Of

◇◇◇◇◇◇ ◇◇◇◇◇◇◇◇◇
◇◇◇◇ ◇◇◇◇ ◇◇◇◇◇◇.
◇◇◇◇◇◇◇ ◇◇ ◇◇◇◇.
◇◇◇◇◇◇ ◇◇ ◇◇◇◇.

THIS IS NOT FROM HER. This is from me.

From the hands that built you and the hands that broke you.

I was supposed to save you.

When I wrote you, I laced you with hope, even when you didn't know how to wear it. I threaded pieces of myself into your silence, your kindness, your cruelty. I built you from the grief I didn't know how to name, from the longing that lived under my ribs like a second pulse. You were supposed to be flawed. You were supposed to stumble. But you were supposed to make it.

You were supposed to be the boy who survived.

Instead, I buried you.

I put the bullet in your story and the dirt over your name.

I wrote your death with my own hands, and when I closed the chapter, something in me closed too.

You loved with a recklessness you didn't know how to tame.

You held your hurt inside your mouth like it was something sacred.

You made yourself small so others could feel larger.

You lived your life trying to be less than the damage written into your bloodline.

You were not innocent.

You were not pure.

But you deserved the chance to become something more than the sum of what was done to you.

I took that from you.

Because the story asked for blood, and I gave it yours.

Because the ending needed a body, and I laid down yours.

Because the girl needed a villain, and I let her carve your face into the mask.

I'm sorry I made you the place where all the grief had to end.

You deserved a hand to pull you out of the fire.

You deserved a future you didn't have to fight tooth and bone for.

You deserved more time.

You deserved more mercy.

You deserved to grow old without the weight of every broken thing crashing down on your head.

You deserved a life where your mistakes didn't define you.

I don't forgive myself for writing your end.

Not today.

Not tomorrow.

Maybe not ever.

You were not a casualty.

You were not a plot point.

You were the heartbeat underneath all of it.

You were the boy who built a lighthouse out of broken stones and waited for someone to come home to it.

And in the end, no one did.

I will miss you with every word I ever try to write after this.

I will carry the guilt of you the way some people carry scars across their skin: not as punishment, but as proof that something mattered once.

You are not forgotten, Alexei.

Not by me.

Not by the pages you bled through.

Not by the girl who loved you until she killed you.

Not by the hands that wrote you and failed you.

Sleep well, lighthouse boy.

You deserved to be saved.

And I am sorry I couldn't.

- Eliza.

www.ingramcontent.com/pod-product-compliance
Lightning Source LLC
Chambersburg PA
CBHW060640260626
47161CB00008B/2929